Santino ... , and his star sign ...
He ... at Coventry University (formerly Lanchester Polytechnic School of Art and Design).

In 1980 he went to Milan, northern Italy, where he worked in design; by 1983 he had returned to Coventry and continued design work.

He relocated to Sicily, Italy, in 1986, where his parents originated, and worked in tourism.

TREPIDATION

'I love you, don't forget it'
'I love you, don't forget it'
'I love you, don't forget it'
'I love you, don't forget it'
'I love you, don't forget it'
'I love you, don't forget it'
'I love you, don't forget it'
'I love you, don't forget it'

TREPIDATION

Santino Nerelli

ATHENA PRESS
LONDON

TREPIDATION
Copyright © Santino Nerelli 2006

All Rights Reserved

No part of this book may be reproduced in any form
by photocopying or by any electronic or mechanical means,
including information storage and retrieval systems,
without permission in writing from both the copyright
owner and the publisher of this book.

ISBN 1 84401 588 2

First Published 2006 by
ATHENA PRESS
Queen's House, 2 Holly Road
Twickenham TW1 4EG
United Kingdom

Printed for Athena Press

Contents

Consternation	9
Departure	11
Northbound	16
Rome	31
Milan	70
Paris	83
Reunion	137
Cherbourg	144
Ireland	154
Southbound	167

Consternation

Luca decided that, after a year of hard work in the hotel, he was going to take a holiday. After careful thought and contemplation he decided to visit the green island of Ireland.

He was a night porter, working in a small twenty-six-room hotel. His work season was from April to February. It was sixteen years or more since he had taken a holiday, since he had left the island of Sicily.

As he was not a regular long-distance traveller, and not a lover of the aeroplane, his journey to Ireland would be by train.

Going on holiday may seem a simple thing to do, but not for this man.

The decision to go was reached with extreme difficulty. He could not see himself outside his Sicilian island home. He tried every night to imagine himself making all the preparations, getting the suitcase, placing it on the bed and then systematically going through all his clothing needs. How many trousers, jumpers, shirts and underpants to take? It would be a very simple task to most people, but it was difficult for Luca. He thought too much and weighed up the utility of each and every item. So before say, a jumper was included, he would first have to see if it was still in good condition; to see if it was not too old, with holes. Then he would try it on, to check that he hadn't grown out of it. He would compare the jumper with the others in his collection, to see if the chosen one was the best colour, design, size, thickness or material. He would consider and compare them all, and then through a process of elimination he would choose. He hated travelling or preparing for journeys. So before he actually set off, his imagination of everything related to the trip created a fear in him – a fear of the unknown, fear of a change in his routine.

He then imagined himself on the ferry. He could see himself climbing on to the ramp with his luggage, and already he was worried about where he would sit. Every step of the way seemed to create a phobia in his mind.

He even worried about what would happen if he couldn't find an empty seat on the train, if the toilets would be clean or not. He worried if he would find a place to sleep at night on the train, or in one of the many stations. He worried too about missing train connections and thus remaining stranded in stations. He worried about not feeling well on the way, about getting bad headaches or even heart attacks. There would be no home comforts and no help from family members.

The journey ahead, for Luca, was not a simple one. This simple journey was comparable to a rocket journey to the moon. He felt that it was full of danger, yet somehow he knew he had to go through with it. It was like stage fright. There he was, at one end of the journey, with a towering, invisible mental wall to climb: the wall of fear.

Departure

It was a telephone conversation with his former girlfriend, Katherine, from Ireland that made him decide to make the journey. She was very upset to hear that he was refusing to get on a train to make the long journey north. He could hear her crying at the other end, and suddenly the telephone line carried a different weight. The sound of her crying was like an imaginary long arm and hand reaching out over 2,000 kilometres from her in Ireland to him in Sicily. The sound of her tears gave him the impetus to make a go of it and depart.

A few minutes after putting the phone down, Luca put his luggage in the boot of the car and drove to the village railway station. He parked the car and handed over the car keys to his mother and then proceeded to the platform to wait for the train to take him on his first stage of the journey to nearby Messina. There were only a few commuters waiting for the train, which was exactly on time. As it drew slowly into the station, he kissed his mother goodbye. The train slowly came to a halt, and Luca grabbed his luggage and climbed into the carriage. He walked along the narrow corridor, found a vacant seat, stored his luggage safely on the vacant seat beside him, and stood at the window to wave at his mother, who was still standing on the station platform. Once all the train doors were shut, and all the new passengers on board, the train slowly

Departure

made its way out of the station, on its way to Messina.

The journey to the provincial capital only took forty minutes.

Once the train stopped in Messina, Luca got off with his suitcase (which had small wheels) and sports bag. He made his way to the waiting area, where other people were waiting in a small queue, ready to get on to the ferry. It was a fine, clear, sunny, day. He was almost regretting it. He could be peacefully sitting on the beach, reading his book, or fishing. He could have spent the whole morning relaxing at home; instead he was beginning to get stressed, just beginning a long journey.

The sea seemed very calm. The short thirty-minute crossing was going to be smooth; no rough waves this time. On other occasions the crossings were gruelling as the sea would pitch the ship from side to side.

The short queue made its way on to the ship. Not far from the queue of foot passengers there was a line of cars and lorries waiting to be allowed on by the ferry personnel.

Luca and the rest of the passengers made their way on to the ramp, the same ramp that the motor vehicles used. Once on board, some people went up to the upper decks; only a few passengers, including Luca, stayed on the same deck as the motor vehicles. As it was only a thirty-minute crossing, Luca thought it was not worth climbing the steps to the higher decks, carrying his luggage. It was better to just stand by the cars and lorries and wait those thirty minutes. It meant of course they had to subject themselves to the wind. So Luca found himself somewhere where he'd be

Departure

protected from the strong wind, but still in a place where he could have a good view.

When the passengers and vehicles were all on board, the ship started to move. The engines could be heard and the propellers were churning the water.

The ship slowly moved out of the port. Messina was in full view. It looked like a picture postcard taken from the sea. The further the ship moved out, the prettier the view appeared. Luca could see the undulating Peloritani Mountains taper out to the wide, panoramic, blue Mediterranean Sea, and disappear behind the vibrant busy and noisy city of Messina. He could distinguish the city buildings with their big neon signs and the numerous noisy city cars racing up and down the major seaside road. He could observe other ferry vessels parked in the port, some taking on motorcars and foot passengers, some taking on the train, after it had been sectioned into smaller carriages to fit the ferry ship. He could focus on the statue of the Madonna, situated at the Messina port entrance, looking similar to the Statue of Liberty in New York.

On the same deck there was another man, a much older man. He too was alone, with a suitcase, dressed in ordinary clothes, with a typical Sicilian cap on his head and a scarf around his neck.

He seemed to be having some difficulty with his suitcase. He too could not be bothered to climb the narrow metal steps from the car deck to the upper passenger deck. The suitcase was too cumbersome or heavy for him to handle.

Luca, having spotted the old man, decided to approach him and ask if he needed any help. Apparently, he didn't need any help, but it quickly became obvious that he wanted someone to keep him company. So for the remainder of the crossing of the straits of Messina, Luca decided to stay near the old man. Together they watched the town of Messina getting smaller and smaller and receding into the distance.

After a brief introduction, the old man told Luca that he was going north to visit his son, who had been living in the north of Italy since he had left his parental home in Messina.

The crossing was soon over. The ferry was now at Villa San Giovanni, a port at the tip and toe of the long boot of Italy. Debarkation was quick and easy. The old man stayed quite close to his new-found companion. Both men found their way to the railway station, where they were going to catch the train that would take them to Rome.

On arriving at the station, they made their way to a small bar, which was beside the railway station. The old man wanted something to drink and offered Luca a drink but he didn't want anything. After a quick coffee, the two men made their way to the platform, where the train to Rome was due to arrive.

They both sat on a marble bench and checked that they had their tickets. All they had to do now was wait.

The wait was a long one. Trains came in and out of the station, but none of them was the train to Rome. It was delayed as usual. Already, Luca was concerned. His ticket was already booked and paid for from Messina to Paris, but the tickets didn't guarantee that the trains would be on time. A delay in the departure from Messina or from Villa San Giovanni or any delay

Departure

along the way would mean the possibility of missing the next train at Rome, the train that would take him to Paris.

Luca was worried. He started to envisage himself staying in the station in Rome, lying on a bench.

After thirty minutes the train came into the station. It was half an hour late. Luca was now sure that, at this rate he was going to miss the connection in Rome.

The train came to an abrupt stop. Both men got up, made their way to the train carriages, and said goodbye to each other, as each had a different seat number. All seats on this train were reserved.

Northbound

Luca climbed the steps on to the train. He placed his suitcase on the rack then made his way to find his reserved seat. There were not that many people getting on the train, so it was easy to walk through the gangway with his sports bag and find his reserved seat. His number was 113. He placed his bag on the rack above the seats, and then tried to make himself comfortable.

The train was running late. Luca sat near the window. He always chose to sit near the window, as he loved looking out at the fast moving scenery. As yet, there was no other passenger sitting in his section of the train. He opened his bag and pulled out a bottle of water, had a drink and put the bottle back in the bag.

The station guard waved his paddle towards the front of the train, and with a jolt the train slowly started to move.

Luca had left home at seven in the morning, and now it was already five in the afternoon. It had taken all this time to travel a few miles. *Madness!* With a plane, one would have taken but a few hours to get to one's destination. Instead, Luca, due to his fear of flying, had chosen to take the slower route.

Once he'd settled down on the train he gazed out of the window. He could see the Mediterranean Sea close by. He was used to the sea, as he had been living by it for the last eighteen years, since he had gone to live in Sicily. But as he sat on the train, the sea seemed to be crying out to him, crying out and saying goodbye to him. The sea was saying, 'See you soon, go, have your break, but see you soon…'

The train gathered momentum. Luca looked out of the window, and not only could he see the blue sea but also the villages with all their different houses and gardens. The sea seemed to be one continuous mass, but the houses and all that was on land seemed to fly by at a growing speed: trees, houses, cars, roads, schools, fields, bridges, tunnels, farms, ponds, rivers, all started to whisk by. That's what Luca liked about travelling by train. So many different things could be seen in a few seconds; and he liked the high speed that the train travelled at. Yes, Luca was afraid to set foot outside his home, he was afraid to buy a train ticket, he was afraid of the whole idea of travelling; but now that he was sitting there comfortably, all organised, he just loved to watch the view flash past the train window.

It was a bright sunny day and still no one had got on the train to share his compartment. For how long would he have the seats to himself? He knew that sooner or later the compartment would fill with strangers, and he would have no choice but to break his beloved silence and isolation. The ticket inspector, dressed in his uniform, came in, asked to see his ticket, and then carried on down the corridor.

The train kept on gathering speed until it was going very fast. A black screen regularly interrupted the beautiful scenery out of the window. The train was speeding through the many tunnels and each time it went through one, the bright light entering the train cabin was chopped off, as if the electricity mains supply had been switched off; this went on for miles. The traveller opened his cabin window, and each time the train charged into the black tunnel, the compressed air made such a loud thud that it gave the impression that the train had crashed into something – another train perhaps. Yes, the thought did cross his mind, the possibility of having a train crash, the possibility of hitting another train travelling in the opposite direction – possibly in the middle of one of the many dark long tunnels. What a disaster it would be! Still, he thought, it would be slightly less disastrous than a plane crash; there are usually no survivors after a plane crash. So it was only at the entrance of the long tunnels that Luca became fearful of travelling. It was at that moment he would think about being back at home in his seaside village, sitting on the beach in front of the sea, watching and listening to the water caressing and lapping the stony shore.

It was too late now. He and his luggage were already miles from Villa San Giovanni, on the tip of Italy, and the train was progressively making its way north.

It was great for Luca to have the whole compartment to himself. He could put his feet up on the seat opposite, or even lie down and stretch out. He had brought a small radio with him, tucked away in his sports bag. Just in case he became bored, he could listen to it, to the conversations that were often broadcast – he loved talk shows – but he would most likely stare out of the window, and he often fell into deep thought. His thoughts would swing from one topic to another... thoughts about his life, the good and bad aspects. He would think about his past, his future, and he would think about the good and bad times. He had plenty to keep him busy, with his thoughts. Many people buy magazines or books to read on journeys, but Luca preferred to wander in his mind.

The train had to stop eventually, and on came the first passengers, also travelling to Rome. His compartment was empty one moment, and the next moment it was full. A family of three generations came into the cabin: grandmother, daughter and grandson, all three occupied the seats opposite Luca. They were well dressed; they said 'Hello' to Luca and made themselves comfortable. The young woman had very long dark hair; she was quite striking; her son seemed fidgety and noisy. It looked as if Luca was going to have some disturbance ahead, especially from the boisterous boy.

Other people were going up and down the corridor, trying to find a seat in the nearby compartments.

A man with a Neapolitan accent was walking along the corridor. He was carrying a transparent plastic bag; he was trying to sell his home-made sandwiches to the passengers. The sandwiches were all neatly packed close together in the bag; the sandwich man didn't look very clean and tidy. His unshaven face and casual and dirty looking clothes were sure to put off anyone buying his sandwiches, or rather, *panini*. When the sandwich man stuck his head in the cabin, everyone ignored him; nobody would dare buy a sandwich from him, neither Luca nor the three new passengers in the compartment. The sandwich man waited a few seconds, then left.

How can you do business like that? Luca thought to himself; how can you expect someone to buy food from you if you look shabby? Perhaps the Neapolitan hadn't realised that the train had a clean, well-furnished restaurant/bar in one of the carriages. Luca thought back to a man in Taormina who sometimes tried to sell his red roses to the tourists in the street. He, too, dressed in an unsuitable way, unshaven too. Luca remembered a brief encounter he'd had once with the flower seller outside the hotel entrance. He had sold no roses and was in a bitter mood. The flower seller had stopped outside the hotel where Luca worked as a night porter, and could be seen playing rough with a kitten, harming it. The porter had asked him to leave the kitten alone. The short, shabby, unshaven flower seller had come up to the porter with a menacing face-to-face stare and with a threatening, raucous voice said to him, 'Watch it, stay out of my way, because one of these days I will kill you!' Luca never forgot the episode and could never understand why the other man had taken against him. After the incident, the porter made sure he kept a good distance from the flower seller. They often walked the same central street in Taormina, and Luca made sure he avoided his possible assassin; the flower vendor did after all have that Mafia look and air about him.

It's normal, from Rome down to Sicily, to see men rushing up and down the station platform with their trolleys full of sandwiches or drinks, trying to sell their goods to the thirsty or hungry train passengers through the open train windows. It's also normal to see them get on the train whilst it's stationary in the station, and take their supplies directly into the cabins, trying to do business and compete with the train's restaurant. Alas, some of them have no idea of how to present their merchandise. They look and dress as if they are more worn out than the passengers.

The passengers opposite Luca, the two women and the little boy, were well dressed, and also well stocked with their own food and drinks. The porter himself only had to reach out into his bag to get at his cheese and ham sandwiches.

It was approximately one o'clock, and once all the other passengers had finished getting on the train, pushing and pulling their luggage through the narrow corridor, and finding their reserved seats in the second-class section, the porter got his sandwiches out and started to eat. The two women opposite him soon did the same.

The train started to move again. Slowly it gathered pace, and within a few minutes it was travelling again at full speed.

The porter was still a little concerned that the train would be late reaching Rome. There was nothing he could do about it now; he was already miles from home and he was halfway to Rome. The journey from Sicily to Rome usually takes about eight hours. Outside the window on the left, the sea could be seen, and on the right there were mountains.

At another station, an old woman entered the compartment with her tall and sturdy son. They sat in the two remaining seats, and the porter noticed that the woman was dressed in black from head to toe. They talked to each other in a language that wasn't Italian; it was Sicilian dialect, which is quite different. They looked like each other: both had dark skin and dark black eyes. They started talking to each other, ignoring the remaining passengers. Gradually the conversation became heated; it was almost a public argument. The old woman started to get angry about something, and the son was getting angry that his mother was getting angry; their voices became raised. It was not easy to understand the basis of their discontent, as their language was incomprehensible to the others in the cabin. Most people usually understood the dialect of their own region. So the old woman and her fiery-tempered son continued arguing for a while. They were making the other passengers very uncomfortable, but after about five minutes they calmed down. The old woman seemed to go into a quiet trance or sulk, as if defeated by her much bigger and stronger son.

The porter could imagine the son in his own home. He thought up a scene in which the son sat with family and friends at the dinner table, about to enjoy the food, when suddenly the son crashed his clenched fist down, hard and fast onto the table, making a loud thunder, shaking the table and house foundations as if in an earthquake, rattling all the plates and glasses, startling the seated and suddenly muted family and friends, then, saying in an angry brute style growl, 'This pasta is too salty, this pasta is for the bin!' Suddenly the silenced family and friends, shocked by the sudden unexpected outburst, probably enjoying the meal, would suddenly be made to feel awkward, bad and so terribly nervous and uncomfortable, and uneasy about continuing and finishing their dinner, which, in everyone's silent opinion was food that was in reality quite edible.

The porter could imagine the old woman with her long pointed nose and bulging black eyes waving a long, old wooden walking stick, like a musketeer, at anyone who ventured near the front door of her house.

It was getting dark outside and the lights in the train had been switched on. The train continued to accelerate, to go faster and faster, in an attempt to catch up on lost time.

The porter watched the long train, carriage after carriage, disappear under the mountain into a tunnel. He asked himself how much work and effort went into the construction of all these tunnels. He imagined and visualised the builders at work, with their excavating machinery. He could see the sweat running off their foreheads.

His thoughts then turned to the great tunnel built under the English Channel, the great engineering and construction masterpiece, built, for the first time, under the sea; and then his thoughts leapt to the near future, the future of the straits of Messina, with its new long bridge which would connect the island of Sicily with the mainland of Italy.

The train slowed down and stopped. They were somewhere near Naples. It was already dark outside, but the station was well lit. There were a few policemen around, walking in twos, with their hands behind their backs. The family of three grabbed hold of their belongings and left the train. The little boy, who was with his attractive young mother and grandmother, had not caused any trouble after all.

Not far from Naples is one of Europe's most famous volcanoes, Vesuvius – another reason for fear.

Although the volcano is dormant today, it's still a volcano. It reminded Luca of his own close encounters with a volcano, Etna, in Sicily. He had first been to visit Europe's biggest volcano when he was fourteen years of age, to explore the craters which were, at the time, dormant. He could remember his last happy outing with his father that summer, before his father died. Then he thought of the volcano's destructive nature, the time that the volcano made front page news in the national newspapers, with its dangerous lava flows that destroyed everything in its path.

Luca's closest encounter with the mighty mountain was quite recent. Whilst at work one night, in his hotel and sitting on his armchair in the hall at about 3 a.m., he had felt the earth tremble beneath his feet. His chair had shook for a minute or so, and it was a clear indication that a few miles beneath him, the earth was moving. It was hot, and it was lava; it was surely a frightening experience. The hotel, situated in the pretty town of Taormina, was only a few miles away from the majestic volcano. Could an eruption from Etna ever reach the municipality? Could it ever destroy the houses and hotels of this tourist haven?

One morning the porter had been astonished to find the entrance path to the hotel covered in black dust. He had walked out on to the main street and found that the black sand was everywhere. Everything had been covered in black and grey sand; buildings, gardens, roads, cars, his vehicle included. All was covered in a dark blanket, as far as the eye could see. He had to be careful to wipe the black dust off the windscreen of his car, so as not to leave any scratch marks on the glass. If it were ordinary sand, which is often carried over by the wind and clouds from the Sahara Desert in Africa, it could be easily wiped off without causing any damage. But the black dust coughed up by the volcano contains minute particles of minerals, which scratch glass.

Everywhere had been covered in this black blanket. Luca looked towards the majestic Mount Etna and saw a colossal plume of gray and white smoke rising from the tip of the volcano pyramid, surging from one of the craters to reach high into the crystal clear blue sky; smoke, fumes and gas, undulating high above the mountains and the sea, created an enormous, conspicuously threatening cloud. The beach had looked so peculiar coated in black. The eruption had shot so high into the atmosphere that the wind and clouds had transported the dust particles for miles around. Many of the locals could not remember a similar occasion in the past. They were advised to wear paper masks to shield their mouths and noses; to protect themselves from breathing the volcanic particles into their lungs.

Luca was glad that his home in Sicily was not too close to the volcano Etna, glad that it was highly unlikely his dwelling would on any account be engulfed by the red hot lava. His last visit to the volcano had been a pleasant one, a drive by car to the nearby summit, which was covered in snow, was comparable to driving in Switzerland. There were bendy roads with tall pine trees on either side, with a chalet-style restaurant near the top. The most surprising aspect was the presence of the snow. Normally, during the winter months it covered the whole mountain, but in the spring and summer, it was odd to see the snow when the rest of the island was baking under a hot sun.

Well, at the present Luca was not afraid of the volcano. There was no need to be, as Vesuvius had been dormant for years.

The train was on its way again. The next stop was probably Rome. The old woman and son had quietened down now; they were not quite as explosive as a volcano. The ticket inspector came by and punched a small hole in the train tickets that the passengers were asked to display.

The train accelerated. Now it was dark outside; all that could be seen was some occasional street lamps, or car lights, but it was difficult to see what was outside, as the glass of the train window reflected back into the cabin the internal image, so it was possible for Luca to pretend he was looking outside, but in reality he could sit and stare at his two cabin companions without being noticed. There was something about the pair that he didn't like. He was not a great judge of character, but the simple fact that the two had raised their voices had put them both on a bad footing with him.

The further north the train travelled, the fewer tunnels it went through, a clear indication that the mountains of the south were being left behind. As there was less to see outside the train window, Luca grabbed hold of his sports bag and rummaged through it for a bottle of water and a sandwich. He also tried to see if he could get a radio station on his small portable radio, after placing the earpiece in his ear.

There was nothing on the radio – no music, no talk shows. The reception was bad, so he just ate and drank. He looked at his mobile phone and saw that there was a poor network, that no one had sent him a message. No one from his home in Sicily or from Ireland had yet bothered to communicate with him. He was already feeling isolated and alone, and again a little afraid. Why was he so afraid on this train? Why was being alone on a train, miles from home, making him anxious? He had travelled the route many times in his life, but he'd never felt this uneasy. Was it the fact that he was now an older person? Some people say you lose courage with age, not just your hair and teeth and memory. Was it simply the fact that he hadn't travelled for so long? Had living on an island for such a long stretch of time turned him into a prisoner – a prisoner to himself? Why did he feel like a solitary navigator at sea, alone in a rowing boat? Why did he feel he was sailing towards the unknown, or to an imaginary cliff or waterfall at the edge of the ocean?

The sea was no longer in sight. There was a long silence – apart from the noise of the train, of its wheels clattering rhythmically every time they rolled over railway track joints. Luca had often thought, Why doesn't someone make a musical soundtrack with the sound of the railway? He reckoned it had probably been done before.

No conversation had been initiated between Luca and his fellow travellers. If their eyes met, a reciprocal smile would merely be switched on. Luca reached out for a newspaper that was lying on a seat, and started to look at the pages, firstly at the photographs, then at the titles. Reading was never his forte, but boredom had now pressed him to read. Occasionally, he would glance at the reflection in the window to see what the old woman and her son were up to.

More time had elapsed, and more distance had been travelled. The appearance of city lights in the distance meant that the train was approaching Rome. Another glance at his wristwatch told him that the train had not arrived on time. Would his train connection to Paris still be there in the station? He was doubtful. In the past, Luca had travelled to England by train without any problems, he would buy the ticket and be certain to arrive; train travel was probably more popular and better organised in those days. Today, most people travel long distances by plane, so a long-distance voyage by train is not set out in the brochures or planned by travel agents. A long train journey today means taking a certain risk. The chances of getting stuck in a station overnight are high, and it seemed likely that this was going to happen on this occasion. The thought began to preoccupy him. Where would he spend the night? Why hadn't he just got on a plane? All these hours sitting on a train could have been avoided.

Friends and family had all told him often to take to the air. He would be at his destination in a few hours, rather than spending all this time on trains and boats, and in railway stations; but no, for a few years now, Luca would not get on a plane. The last time he'd attempted it, he pulled back at the last minute, therefore forfeiting his flight ticket; again the element of fear had struck him. The thought of getting into a heavy machine and being unnaturally lifted into the sky terrified him. The loud roar of the jet engines; the vibrating race down the runway; the sudden increase in speed, the sudden change of angle; the engines' impulsive thrust and increased power to push the heavy metallic bird off the ground and towards the sky; the steady increases in height and distance from the ground; the gradual diminishing views of terra firma; the increase in the emptiness and space beneath him.

His fear of flying was probably fed by the fact he watched too many disaster movies, and only recently he had watched a documentary on Italian TV, about technical failures on aeroplanes, with cargo doors ripping off and explosions due to possible short circuits. Of course, not only could the plane be at fault, but the people who flew in them; in particular hijackers, terrorists or suicide pilots and bombers. So, although they had often told Luca that it was the safest way to travel, sitting on an aeroplane seat meant subjecting himself to hours of nail-biting fear and terror. There have been many air disasters, and, when one does happen, most passengers perish. However, Luca had often been in contact with people who flew on planes. Clients coming to his hotel travelled great distances – from Australia, from China or Japan – and none of them ever complained of their long journey. The concierge thought to himself that one day he would have to face the fear head-on, and fly. He wouldn't be able to travel long distances by land for ever; he'd get tired of it some day.

The train was now entering Rome Station; everybody was getting ready to get off. Heavy suitcases were lifted off the racks, and everyone began putting their coats on, as the temperature seemed to have dropped as night approached. Luca grabbed hold of his suitcase and sports bag and made his way out of the compartment into the corridor. He looked at his travelling companions and gestured a goodbye with his eyebrows, and happily left them. Luca struggled a while along the corridor, passing by other passengers, making his way to the train door. Pulling and pushing, he eventually made his way off the train and on to the station platform. Luca just hoped that the train for Paris had been delayed. He started to make his way to the head of the train. It was a long walk to the main platform, to the ticket office, bar and waiting area. It was useful to have a suitcase with small wheels; still, pulling all this weight was causing him to heat up. He hurriedly looked for the information desk and queued up behind other foreign nationals. He was impatient; sweat began to pour down his face. After twenty minutes of anxious waiting, it was his turn to face the information and ticket desk.

Rome

Luca had missed the train by twenty minutes. The woman behind the desk advised him to go and get a refund and buy a new ticket to Paris, which he promptly did. However, this time it was obligatory for him to change train at Milan; the only other inconvenience being that he had to stay in Rome overnight.

Where would he stay? It was 10 p.m. and the train to Milan was at nine the next morning. With his new ticket tucked away in his pocket and luggage at hand, he stood outside the terminal building wondering what to do. After a few minutes, between looking around, eating another sandwich and considering his options, he came to a decision. He either slept in the station, or in a hotel. His third and last option was to get in touch with a friend, Antonio, who lived and worked in Rome somewhere. He decided to phone him. He dialled the number and hoped it was the right one. His old friend was glad to hear from him, but he seemed to have a rough voice; Antonio invited him to stay at his flat, to make his own way by following his directions. All Luca had to do was get on the underground and get off at the last station. Antonio would meet him at the exit.

Luca hadn't seen Antonio for a very long time. They were more or less the same age. Antonio was a qualified psychiatrist, and had a good job. Luca remembered him from his childhood days when they used to play together. He also remembered the difficult upbringing he had, especially with his father, who often beat him with a belt if he didn't do his homework, if he didn't learn the alphabet or multiplication tables. Luca and his friend had also spent a lot of time on the beaches of Sicily, trying to chat up the tourists.

Antonio invited him up to his flat. Apparently he was staying in his girlfriend's flat. It was in a nice part of Rome, but the apartment on the top floor was a very small one. The state of the flat was not very clean. In the kitchen it seemed that the dishes hadn't been done for weeks. There were dirty plates and pans everywhere. The bins were all full to the brim. Luca was astonished to see that Antonio was living in such conditions. Books were scattered everywhere in an untidy mess. Had Antonio or his girlfriend gone loopy? Was he depressed? Didn't he have the time to clean up? Was he so busy at work? Luca didn't ask, just wondered.

Luca had a shower. He needed one – he had been sweating profusely since getting off the train. Then, afterwards he could sit and talk to Antonio about the good old days. Whilst eating his home-made meatballs in tomato sauce, his friend started firing questions at him. Where was he going? Why was he going to Ireland?

After a long talk at the table, Antonio showed him the view of Rome from his balcony. Houses with gardens on their rooftops could be seen all around – an amazing sight!

It was about one o'clock when they decided to go to sleep, and Luca was shown his bedroom. How glad he was to have a bed to lie on, and not a make-do deck-chair type of bed, packed with sponges, like he had at work. Not that he had to sleep at work, but he was allowed to rest during quiet hours in an armchair. So, at work, Luca tried to improvise a bed; but a real bed was better. He learnt to appreciate the bed and the night.

He learnt to appreciate that the night is best used for sleeping, so he was definitely delighted to have a bed for the hours of darkness.

In the bedroom, the bed looked inviting, but horror posters covered the walls. Antonio's girlfriend's brother was into fear-provoking images. So before Luca settled down to sleep, he looked at these pictures on the wall. There were witch-like women and alien monsters looking down at him. Was another night going to be a sleepless one for Luca? Was he not yet free to sleep in peace?

For eighteen years it had always been a bit of a battle to get a decent night's (or day's) sleep, but ultimately it was hell. Getting into bed in the morning at his home in Sicily, his next-door neighbour would hammer on his walls, sometimes with a hammer, sometimes with a drill, and the noise would be intolerable; it would go on for hours. Luca often felt like getting out of bed, wearing only his pants, grabbing hold of a Mafia-style, short-barrelled *lupara* shotgun (if he'd had one), and going out into the street. He'd go into the house next door, and gun down whoever was making that noise on the walls with the drill or hammer. The noise in his bedroom was intolerable, unbearable. The continuous banging of the walls only seemed amplified when he was tired and had been up most of the night, and Luca would easily get nervous or bad-tempered.

He also thought how inconsiderate his neighbours were. They knew he worked nights, yet they went ahead with their do-it-yourself building work. Luca wouldn't have minded if the work only took a few days, but it went on for months. If he notified the *carabinieri* or police, they would surely tell him that there is nothing that they could do about it, as the man was working, drilling and banging in his own home.

On top of the noise next door, Luca had to put up with the noise from the passing trains and cars, for his house was sandwiched between the main road and the railway line.

Lying there on the bed in this small flat in Rome, looking up at the picture of the witch on a broomstick stuck on the wall opposite him, he contemplated his job as a night porter. He thought back to his early beginnings as a twenty-six-year-old unemployed person just arrived in Sicily. He thought back to the various things that had happened and to the people he'd met, there in the hotel reception hall of the small twenty-six-room villa. He thought back to the people he worked with, the nice and the nasty ones.

The poster of the witch on the wall in his bedroom immediately reminded him of an old woman. For some strange reason, Luca had more contact at work and in his neighbourhood with old women than he had with the young. The young sexy women mostly kept their distance out of shyness, but the old were always near him; not that he didn't like old women, but why was he always in their company? Were they his guardian angels?

Rome

He thought back to old Donna Francesca. She was a little old woman who at the age of seventy-five still came to work in the hotel at five o'clock in the morning. At that dark hour of the day, the hotel door was usually locked . The night porter would still sometimes be lying on his spongy deckchair in the little boxroom, adjacent to the entrance hall, trying to sleep another few minutes. Punctually at five, you would hear her approach at the hotel, dragging her feet slowly, and muttering to her cat, named Pépé. She would arrive at the hotel door, which was an old-fashioned wooden double door with loose glass panels in it. She would go for the handle to open the door, but on seeing that it was still locked, she would start to call out for the porter. She'd start to rattle the door, the glass panels would rattle loudly. The old woman would start to shout, '*Luca! Luca!*' as if she was having a sort of panic attack. She would not stop rattling and knocking, or rather banging, on the villa door; she was probably afraid that the porter was dead in the small room.

Luca was always aware of her in the mornings. He didn't need her to wake him up with the loud banging on the door. He would jump up and open the door, and she would come in, followed by the big fat cat, who was a prince to Donna Francesca. Rather than asking the porter if he was all right, she would ask him immediately the number of occupied rooms in the hotel. She wanted to know if Luca had let any more rooms; she would then judge if things were all right. She could tell if business was going well or not going well, and she acted as if the hotel belonged to her, as if she was the proprietor's spokesman. If the numbers of the room were high, all was good; if the numbers were low, then the threats came in, the threat of hotel closure being on the horizon, the threat that the hotel owner would send all the hotel employees home. There was always this intimidation, this fear, that the owner of the hotel would sack everyone if business was not good.

On several occasions the porter argued with the old woman. She made him nervous, but most of the time he tried to keep on good terms with her; after all, there was a generous woman behind that hard façade. Most evenings, when Luca started his night shift at 9 p.m., Donna Francesca would always give him something from the kitchen, usually some yoghurt or a piece of fruit.

When he had first started to work there, the hotel was run by foreign women. The manager was a German woman, and the afternoon staff at the reception were women from Holland and Austria. It was nothing like the comedy of the TV series, *Fawlty Towers*; it was more like living in a military camp. None of the staff seemed very kind, they all behaved as if they detested being there, and they detested the newcomer, the porter. He was treated like a new military recruit – always corrected and shouted at. There was not, and never had been a good feeling in the workplace; it seemed as if the hotel staff were a collection of bad apples. They all had aggressive personalities. Was it the hotel that turned people into aggressive beings, into angry lions, or worse, into evil demons?

Everything the porter did seemed to disagree with the German manager. Notes written with a red biro were often left for Luca to read. It was very much like being in a strict school, an elementary school, the teacher with her pupils. He would be told off for not dusting the reception desk, or failing to clean the hall windows, or even for not cleaning the floor, so he often went home feeling bad and miserable. When he returned to work the next day he was in fact afraid to find another red note; it was surely not the way to be treated by your colleagues. He expected to be treated like an adult, not as a truant at school. The training period was wicked.

It was good enough reason to give up the job and find something better, to find employment where he'd be treated better, but times were hard, and jobs were scarce in Sicily, so whoever had a job stuck to it, whatever the difficulties encountered, whatever the humiliation one had to endure. Rather than look for another job, Luca thought it was best to try and improve his existing workplace. So he endured it, he persevered; after all, deep down he was used to being in the company of hot-headed and bad-tempered people. The job had its positive aspects and the porter was not going to let a bunch of wild women make him run away.

Luca lay there on his bed in Rome and could not sleep. He continued to stare at the witch on the wall, continued to think back to his time at the hotel. He had the lamp on by the side of the bed, so he was not totally in the dark; for him, it was almost like yet another night, in the villa – the mad villa!

The hotel was appealing to most of the tourists who came to stay. They knew little of the goings-on between the staff behind the scenes. As long as the rooms were clean and the breakfast was good, little did they care about anything else. The night porter was there most nights to greet and register all the new and old clients.

He was also there to give the hotel guests general information about the surrounding area. He would offer them his own personal knowledge of places to visit, like Palermo, Agrigento and the Valley of the Temples, of Syracuse, and of Enna and its famous mosaics. He would tell them of the famed Mafia town of Corleone where it is said that the Mafia had originated. He would tell them about Aci Castello and Aci Catena near Catania where you could see giant rocks jut out of the sea, said to be the rocks thrown by the legendary giant, the one-eyed Cyclops.

The porter in particular gave them information concerning the Messina to Catania region. He would tell them to visit Catania and the pretty port town of Messina, to visit not only the famous cathedral with its famous external gold mobile statues that moved every hour, but also to go watch and enjoy the spectacular, colourful picturesque ferryboats go in and out of Messina Port, with Reggio Calabria, the tip of mainland Italy in the background, only three kilometres away across the straits of Messina.

He would tell them about all the seaside villages along the coast, Ali Terme, Nizza di Sicilia and Roccalumera. He would tell them of Furci Siculo, where local fresh fish stalls sell an abundant variety of Mediterranean fish, including the enormous Swordfish with its long sword-like nose, and its great big black penetrating eyes. He would mention the town of Santa Teresa di Riva, the alluring village of Sant Alessio and the dominating municipality of Forza D'Agró situated 400 metres above sea level, from where you can see a spectacular panorama of the area below, the Sicilian coastal hiss and mountains, the seaside villages together in a row, one after the other; the Mediterranean sea, and the mountains of mainland Italy in the distance.

Luca would passionately recommend they go and watch the most spectacular, colourful, heart-warming early morning sunrise ever seen, ever created by Nature's magically creative flair; to watch the sun's reflection glimmer on the sea's surface, creating a kaleidoscope of colours; to admire the changing colours of the orange and blue sky as the sun slowly rose like a gigantic red eye; and to gape at the high-flying jets and their smoky trails fading across the face of the fading moon, or to gaze at the last flicker of the disappearing stars, or planets, like Venus, Saturn and Mars.

Luca would tell them to go to Forza D'Agró, the 'historic' village, to see some very old and abandoned houses dominated by the ancient Saracen castle, to see the village where time seems to have stopped and now inhabited by a few old individuals. 'It's the village where some scenes from *The Godfather* were recorded,' the porter proudly informed them. He would recommend they go cycling, jogging, horse-riding, or simply walking along the mountain trails, to breathe the true

Mediterranean scented air between lemon, orange, mandarin, orange, almond and corpulent juicy fig trees, but would urge them to be careful not to pick from the spiky cactus plant which generates the prickly-skinned but succulent fruit.

Luca would tell his guests to visit Savoca, another amiable village and *Godfather* film location, to see the fascinating burial chamber where upright medieval mummies of local priests and noblemen might be looked at in awe. There they would see the skulls and clothed skeletons, the living facing the dead, face to face, only inches apart, see their dried out hands and veins, their laughing teeth and jaws, their desiccated genitals, stand there in front of an upright cadaver and ponder on who they were, what kind of life they lived, and whether they were happy in their lives. There, one could look straight into their empty eye sockets and wonder if they were happy now, wherever their spirits may be, or whether they were content to have their earthly decomposed, mummified bodies standing upright, on exhibition in a chamber for all to see?

He would direct them to Giardini Naxos, the first Greek settlement and today a tourist seaside resort, and of course he would tell them the way to see Mount Etna, the overbearing volcanic mountain, responsible for many demonic destructive hell-like lava flows, down along its 3,000 metre slope. He would mention the small volcanic islands off the north coast of Sicily where tourists can bathe in a hot bubbling mud pond. He would also mention the Alcantara Gorges, the cold river surrounded by a rocky landscape, also a bathing area.

Rome

He would give them directions to go and see places in the tourist Mediterranean jewel town of Taormina, in particular to see the ancient Greek/Roman theatre, and ultimately he would indicate to the hotel guests where they could go and eat delicious Sicilian food and listen to live Sicilian folk music.

He was the only staff member on duty at night to keep the hotel running. He was a sort of one-man band; his duties at night were not many. The work was not really that heavy, in the physical sense. At about 9 p.m., or midnight, depending on the hotel's needs, the porter had to be on duty behind the tall grey glass-covered desk. Luca would quickly summarise the situation; he would take note of what needed doing during the approaching night. How many arrivals and departures would there be? At what time would they be expected to turn up or leave? Would there be any wake-up calls?

Once he had the general picture of the situation laid out in his mind, he could settle down, and look forward to a quick short night; it would be quick and short if all the clients would go to their rooms early, and it would be a long, drawn-out night if the clients stayed out late, returning to the hotel at three or four o'clock or at the crack of dawn. For this reason the porter had bought himself a small portable TV. He would get it out of his locked locker, out of its box, place the monitor behind the reception divider near the telephone, then unravel the long extension wire so that it could be plugged in the only socket left for him to use. He might have to stay awake till seven in the morning, so a small TV would be his faithful companion and ally.

Once there had been a big argument regarding the TV plug with the old male manager, who was new to the job. There was a socket for most of the plugs, situated behind the reception. In this one socket most of the plugs were inserted – the computer plug, the printer plug, the fax machine plug. The socket was overloaded, but also loose, so if it was touched by accident, by someone's foot or leg, then everything electronic would go awry. The printer, fax and computer would all have a blackout. Once this did indeed happen, and the porter was blamed. The manager was convinced that Luca had plugged his portable TV into the socket too, thus moving the loose socket and causing an interruption in the electricity supply.

If the computer and printer were out of use, it was a tragedy. How would the hotel clients pay their bills and get their receipts? What chaos there would be if there was a queue of clients leaving at the same time in the morning, all waiting to pay their bills, all of which would have to be written by hand! When the socket was misplaced, it was often difficult to get the electricity supply back again. When this accident happened, the porter was the first to be held responsible. The grumpy old manager had shouted angrily, 'Was it you who messed up the socket and plugs? It was, wasn't it? You and your little TV! You can't use your TV here, is that *clear*?'

After the first incident, Luca made sure he plugged his TV in another socket, well away from the hotel's electronic apparatus.

The padded deckchair and portable TV were the night porter's main apparatus for getting through the night. If the management ever threatened to remove either of them, Luca would not have been able to continue; the TV was his main companion.

Clients in the hotel would come and go through the door, register, and take or return their room keys. Very few would stop and engage Luca in lengthy conversations; it was not a regular occurrence, just a simple, hallo, good evening or goodnight, then up the sixty steps to their rooms.

It was during the winter months that the TV became indispensable. November was generally an extremely quiet month, and not a soul would be around, the hotel would be empty, and no one would be seen or heard outside on the street. You could hear a pin drop in the silence; it would be quiet like a cemetery at night.

On some occasions there would be a raging storm outside, a strong wind making the odd hotel window shutter beat incessantly with rage, and the rain lashing down, creating fast-flowing rivers and floods all around. Sometimes the tremendously loud thunder would shudder the hotel grounds and walls, and the electric bolt-like lightening would strike a nearby tree or tall iron gate, narrowly missing anybody who might have taken the chance of walking under the thundery black, furious sky.

Luca was often alone, with twenty-six empty hotel rooms. The only companion, therefore, was the TV. Luca often felt he wanted to stick his head through it, so as to be in the talk show, or the variety show or in some sexy film. It often felt like pure isolation, isolated from the rest of the world.

Sometimes he would start reading a book, but that would not last for long. If the story were not terribly exciting, he would fall asleep in an upright position, at the risk of losing his balance and falling over behind the reception desk. That would be a great spectacle if a hotel client happened to be around... or it might be dangerous if he fell over and banged his head. Luca sometimes tried to write, but that too made him bored. Reading newspapers kept him occupied for a while, but that couldn't keep him going for ten hours.

Another way of passing the time was drawing. He would get a sheet of A4 paper, usually used for sending faxes, and try to draw, often portraits of women taken from the many old magazines that were lying under the desk. Drawing with pencils kept him busy for two to three hours, but still it made him fall asleep. It was watching TV that would keep him awake for hours, and would help to pass the time more quickly. He could watch an exciting film, or listen to a talk show, which would last well into the night. His job was not physically demanding, but he had to constantly monitor his waking and dozing off time. One minute he could be wide awake; for an hour he could be asleep, then suddenly be woken up by the noise of the door opening, or the telephone ringing. His mind was always half awake and half asleep, as if the two sides of his brain took turns in staying on guard. Most of the night he was aware of what was going on, and any slight noise would make him jump. This constant falling asleep and awakening surely could not be good for him in the long run.

At about 2 a.m., when Luca thought it was highly

unlikely that he would let any more rooms, he would lock the hotel doors and switch most of the lights off, he would make his checks of all the corridors, then he would settle down in his boxroom by firstly clearing away any objects that the day staff might have carelessly left lying around, such as boxes, buckets or even clients' luggage. The room had one of those beds that could be pulled down from the wardrobe and placed in a horizontal position, but the uncaring manager had put a fridge in the room, so that the bed could not be fully opened. The bed could not be used. Not only could the porter not open the bed, but it also had a mattress that had been stuck in it for years. It was mouldy and damp. The manager of the hotel ignored that bed. He didn't want Luca to use the bed; the night porter was to stay awake all the night sitting on a hard armchair in the hotel hall.

Although Luca could not make use of the bed, he had his own, personalized padded deckchair. During the day it was folded away in a black plastic bin liner and left in the room, so when it was late the porter settled his chair in the small room. The place was also used to store cleaning materials, buckets and bottles of detergents, mops, and cloths. It often smelt not only of damp, but also of cleaning liquids, or sometimes even ammonia. When the smell was too pungent, Luca would try to find an alternative solution for his makedo bed, for example trying to fix it in the telephone booth; but that was even smaller than the boxroom, and he really couldn't stretch his deckchair to the full.

The manager often said he could use the deckchair, but only behind the reception desk, or in the middle of the hall. The porter didn't like clients to see him using a deckchair all night; besides, he thought, it would not look good. Placing the chair behind the reception meant dozing off only centimetres away from the, computer, fax machine, telephone and telephone switchboard, and the hotel's electricity supply cupboard with its high voltage wiring. How could Luca doze with his head next to these electronic objects? Luca certainly didn't want brain cancer as well as a wage packet!

Once the chair was unfolded and placed in position, the porter lay on it, often with great relief. Although it was his job to stay awake at night, his biological body clock was telling him it was absolutely time to go to sleep. His body felt heavy and his eyelids drooped. He would leave the room door slightly ajar so that he could keep an eye on the hall. He would be able to hear anyone coming down from his or her rooms in the dead of night, possibly in need of a bottle of water. Hearing the clients' movements as they made their way down the sixty steps from their quarters to the reception hall would usually awaken Luca. It was physically frustrating and stressful to have to force himself awake on demand, at the sound of somebody approaching or wandering in the vicinity. If Luca were halfway to deep sleep, he would have to make a U-turn and come back to the land of the living at the slightest sound, just like a light switch. This continuous falling asleep and awakening put a strain on his mind and hence his whole body.

Most nights were calm, and he would get two or three hours' uninterrupted sleep. On awakening, he would have to switch on the espresso coffee machine, dial a wake-up call to his colleague, the secretary, at her home, to make sure she got to work on time.

Then the porter would do a little cleaning, sweep the floor, and dust around the reception area. At about 7 a.m. he would make his switch with the secretary and then go happily home.

The porter was not always allowed to watch TV and get a few hours' sleep; every night was different. Some nights were very quiet, so there was too much free time; on other nights he wouldn't have time to sit down. The winters were generally very quiet, and summers were very busy.

In winter, the only people in the hotel were ghosts. The hotel, being empty, usually, in November and most of December, allowed room for imagination. Luca thought the hotel was haunted; he would see a beautiful young woman clad in a medieval dress walk through the hotel corridors. She held a candle, and was semi-transparent. Luca would then see her go through doors into the empty hotel rooms – to look for what, he didn't know; but she was beautiful, almost perfect.

He was almost sure the villa was haunted. His childhood nightmare as a consequence at times emerged and haunted him: he could sometimes see a single solitary orb, a single eyeball, like a white moon hovering in the black of space, looking fixedly at him through a keyhole. He could not tell if he was dreaming or if it was real, but he did see her. Each time the dream seemed like reality, so real that sometimes the porter was reluctant to doze off on his deckchair. His encounter with the lady ghost caused him a bit of embarrassment. She would often visit him in his boxroom and inhabit his dreams; she'd make mad passionate love with him, taking on the semblance of a different sexy woman for each visit. It seemed as if the ghost knew every possible erotic situation. It wasn't necessary for the ghost to be in the nude, the naked body was not her method; she invented situations, unlikely situations. She invented a place, an unlikely place and would choose an unlikely moment to molest and arouse Luca. She would take on the semblance of women he knew from the past and present, of women he had never met, as if she had a dictionary of different women and kinds of sex she wanted to perform with Luca, as if she was trying to make him happy in such a rough situation.

Strangely, she would visit him only when he was on his uncomfortable padded deckchair; only when Luca was in the semi-dark hotel boxroom with the door slightly ajar; always punctually at 3 a.m. After hovering and floating down the sixty steps, and entering dauntingly into the boxroom, she would (after sometimes relocating Luca to another setting or scene for his dream), perform sex on the helpless, paralysed, dreaming porter.

Luca would find each and every one of her visits extremely gratifying, overwhelming and uncontrollable, each visit would last a few moments, enough time to satisfy Luca. He would wake up, fully aroused, only to realise it was sadly unreal, just an illusion; but why? Why would he regularly have these ghostly visits? Was the ghost sad and alone? Luca would then wake up, disorientated, embarrassed. He'd sometimes wake up with a dry mouth and a throbbing sensation. It was a good job that no one was around at the time, in the hall, to hear and see the porter lying in the boxroom deckchair, having his profound erotic hallucinations. Sometimes he would wake up with stiff, blood-deprived, rigor-mortis limbs caused by sleeping in an uncomfortable and awkward position.

Working nights often gave him terrible headaches, sometimes excruciating ones; he would often go night after night without getting sleep. Although the winter months were quieter, nights with empty hotel rooms, he did occasionally get the odd client that kept him up the whole night. Luca remembered the time a hotelier from the north of Italy came for a week's holiday with his mother. They were the only clients in the whole hotel, and they were sharing a room. This man would walk down the sixty steps to the hall at three in the morning; he'd engage Luca in conversation and start pacing up and down the hall, up and down, up and down, with his hands behind his back. He would go over the same steps, over and over again, all night long until dawn, until six in the morning, his excuse being that he could not sleep. He told the porter he often paced up and down at night; he said he had something wrong with his brain, that he had had a surgical operation some time ago, and that he was here with his mother on holiday, trying to relax, trying to get away from his own hotel business. The insomniac repeated the night-pacing routine for the whole week. The porter thought to himself that one day he might end up the same, he would end up mad and unable to sleep ever again.

Luca was glad when these lovers of the night paid their hotel bill and left. People who kept him up kept him on duty, and were not desirable. If they kept him up at night-time for too many nights, then the porter would begin to hate them, to see them as enemies, because they were making life unbearable for him.

He particularly disliked the hotel clients who wanted to drink until late, until two, three four or five in the morning. Clients would be sitting in the lounge, laughing out loud, joking and getting drunk and falling on the floor. The porter was not a trained barman, but he was expected to act like one; he was not a waiter, but he had to be one, and he was definitely not a bouncer.

Sometimes during the winter months, as in the summer, some clients might feel unwell and require the porter to call the doctor out. Fortunately in his time there he hadn't needed to deal with real emergencies, or near-death situations, and he hadn't needed to deal with deceased clients. It would have been a problem trying to get rid of a corpse without being noticed; a lifeless person in the hotel would not be good for business.

A dead person would smell after a while, but so far the only pungent odour in the villa occasionally came from the town's main underground drainage system, which smelled a bit like a mushroom factory.

During the winter months, clients would complain of the cold or lack of heat in their rooms, or they might complain of noises from the nearby discothèque, or from the air-conditioning ventilator from another client's room. They might ask for an extra blanket, or simply say they didn't like the view from the room and that they wanted to change it. They would often ask the porter to go up to the room to check the TV and its remote control. Complaints could come at any time during the night, and the porter had to deal with them.

There was once a group of Germans who regularly stayed up late at night to drink beer. They would then stagger to their bedrooms. Once inside, they would continue to shout laugh and make noises, even banging on the walls, and complaints would come from the room next door. On one occasion a client told Luca that the drunk Germans making the noise possessed a small handgun. Was there going to be a murder, a shoot-out at the villa? The drunk Germans soon fell asleep, and probably got sick in the process; that was the end of that small arms episode.

Sometimes clients complained about their partners. One evening Luca was sitting at his desk, quietly watching a film on the TV, when a woman suddenly came down the stairs, sobbing and snivelling. She was distressed, and quickly approached the porter asking him to call the police. She was from London and she insisted that the police be called to come and arrest her so-called boyfriend.

'Look what he has done to my face!' she cried out. 'Look, look!'

Luca saw nothing, but he called the police. When they arrived – and they took a long time to come – they seemed to be unruffled about the woman's distress. The police attached little importance to the whole situation, or appeared to. The porter had to give the woman a separate room. He had to go into her boyfriend's room and get her belongings; he was the go-between, whilst the police limited themselves to writing down her companion's details in a notebook.

The police or *carabinieri* were never called again for other 'disorder' incidents; only the fire brigade were called.

It never really gets very cold in Sicily, the temperature hovers around ten degrees at worst. Still, the hotel had its heating systems. In the lobby there was a Swiss-type stove, made of tiles. It stood on its own with a brass tube going up into the ceiling, which formed its chimney. On entering the foyer, the clients would often stop to admire the green stove. In the winter it would be kept on, therefore hot to the touch, and the clients would lean on it to warm themselves up.

To keep the stove hot, wood has to be put in it, and then lighted. It got very hot, depending on the amount of wood fed into it. On one occasion, and it really was only on one occasion, the porter had to clear out the ash to make way for the new wood. He emptied the ash into an old, empty metal paint bucket, and placed the bucket in the box-room for a moment, which was temporarily filled with stacks of paper, toilet rolls and other things. Luca could not have imagined that he was about to start a little fire in the hotel, minutes before he was due to go home. The ash was practically cold – harmless, or so it seemed. But after half an hour, smoke could be seen coming from the room. The porter opened the door and to his surprise saw the stack of toilet rolls on fire.

He quickly grabbed hold of one of the hotel fire

extinguishers and tried to put the fire out, but unfortunately it didn't work. The fire, once out, would start up again on its own, so Luca hurriedly phoned the fire brigade. They arrived in minutes, and with a hose attached to the water supply, quickly put the fire out. Luca could have been sacked, but the management and owner saw that it was an accident and had not been done intentionally.

Winter in the hotel was not always bad; these incidents were rare. On another occasion, there was a burst pipe in one of the rooms. Luca saw a stream of water running past the main hotel entrance. It was very late at night. He investigated, followed the water back, and found it was coming from one of the rooms. He opened the door, and was taken aback to see the room one metre deep in water. He walked in, soaking his shoes and trousers, and found that water was gushing out of a pipe in the bathroom, under the sink.

When you drive past a hotel you wouldn't believe how many problems can arise in one, and how many things constantly need fixing. The villa had a green book in which the staff used to write down all the faults and broken things that needed repair. Line after line, every day there was always something to fix. 'A new doorknob is needed for Room 23'; 'the tap leaks in Room 30'; 'the water does not drain from the sink in Room 4'; 'the TV does not work in number 12'; 'the fridge makes too much noise in number 24'; 'the air conditioner does not work in Room 5', and so on and so forth.

The list was endless and continuous; the clients paid a lot of money to stay in the hotel, so they always expected perfection. Many clients came down to complain, and it was often the night porter's task to try to solve the problem and to tactfully calm the client. He had to be composed most of the time; he had to smile because the client is always right, and he had to be patient. If he lost his temper, and it did sometimes happen, the client would threaten to leave without paying, or would want to complain to the manager; but the manager would always be on the client's side. Luca had to force himself to be polite most of the time, in every circumstance. He represented the hotel at night, and he always had to give a good impression.

Luca was still staring at the picture of the witch on the wall. He still could not fall asleep, and his mind just continued to wander through his past.

The porter had to be a night watchman too, a kind of policeman. He was there at the entrance all night, not only to register new clients, but also to keep the unregistered people out. In the early days, when he had little experience, he would give the room keys to the right clients, but he would not remember the number of clients in all of the rooms. In the summer, when it was busy and the town was full of tourists, it often happened that young men, registering in the hotel on their own, would go out on the town, sometimes until very late at night, and return with company, usually a woman. The man would take her up to his room without notifying Luca; sometimes he would be with two women. They would walk into the hotel, grab their room keys from behind the reception desk when the porter wasn't there, and hurriedly take the women up to the room. Sometimes homosexuals would sneak a man past the distracted night watchman.

The porter's job was to make sure that only hotel clients stayed the night in their rooms; non-registered persons were illegal and out of bounds. The young man would have his fun with the two women, then, late at night, when Luca had closed the hotel entrance door and gone to lie down on his deckchair, the young man would then come down to the hall with the two women, escorting them out of the hotel.

The porter got into big trouble the first few times the management found out that this had happened. 'You are not to let anybody into the rooms if they are not registered in the book; it absolutely must not happen again, or you will be sacked!' they would say. 'These people must be registered! What if there is a murder? You will be in trouble with the police for not having registered the strangers, is that clear!'

Unregistered clients sometimes slipped past Luca, and when they did, he kept it quiet, or else he would get another telling-off, like a kid at school gets told off by his teacher. On one occasion a homosexual architect asked the porter if he could bring an unregistered man to his room, and only stay a few minutes. Having agreed this with the client, the porter had noted the time, and once five minutes were up, he became uneasy. Ten minutes elapsed, and he felt anxious; after fifteen minutes, Luca was in distress. He now had either to wait a little longer or phone the architect in his room and ask him diplomatically to kindly bring down his cherished guest. So Luca picked up the phone.

'Er, sorry to disturb you, but could you please accompany your guest out of the hotel... he is not registered and must leave. Thank you!'

He must have caught the architect in an awkward moment, because he didn't at all sound too pleased about being hurried out of his room with his friend. Some time later, the architect accompanied his friend down to the lobby, kissed him and waved goodbye. The architect then turned round to the porter and started to get heated up and angry. He accused Luca of being rude and bad-mannered. Luca was astonished to get such a reaction, and tried hard to restrain his own anger.

So it became necessary to keep a vigilant eye on the movements of the hotel clients, to check that no unregistered people sneaked in, and if they were allowed in for five minutes, to check that they left. Luca ended up arguing with a lot of clients, as most of them found the hotel regulations to be absurd.

The porter had to be a traffic warden too. He had to make sure that no cars parked in front of the posh-looking hotel entrance; they would partially hide the view and that would be bad for business. The porter often had to argue with car owners, telling them to move on, not to park there. Sometimes the drivers would end up insulting him, or tell him they would be back in ten minutes. Instead they left the car there until the morning, and that would be another cause for the secretary or her husband, the manager, to lose their tempers with the quiet, submissive worker.

'You have to be more aggressive with people: tell them that you will call the car removers!' they would say, and, 'No one must park their bikes or scooters or

Lambrettas inside the gates; it's absolutely forbidden, is that clear!'

If someone did leave his or her vehicle, car or Lambretta in the hotel entrance, it would always be the porter's fault, and he would never hear the end of it. Parking was scarce in the overcrowded town, especially in the months of July and August, when the place was invaded by thousands of tourists who often brought their own vehicles.

Getting the blame for everything that went wrong had become a normal way of life for the porter. The manager and his wife, approaching their seventies, always pointed the finger at Luca, constantly threatening him with dismissal, even for the simplest things: for forgetting to throw the black refuse bag in the big road bin, or for not correctly taking a room booking over the phone. A simple warning or correction would have been enough, in a civilised, calm manner; but they were hot-headed, and hot-tempered, and they made a big issue over little mistakes. It was absurd, ridiculous, Luca thought.

'Don't take bookings for rooms for one night only over the Christmas week!' they said. The porter forgot the advice given weeks earlier, and did take a booking for one night. The next day he found a note in big block letters: CRETINO, it said. The porter was offended for weeks and weeks. He never forgot the words of the old manager, whom he tried to keep content; it was mere forgetfulness on the porter's part.

There seemed to be no compassion in the hotel. The porter and other staff were expected to work like clockwork, like computers. It would be a serious thing if the porter forgot to make a wake-up call for a client. The client might miss his plane, or excursion; the client would then expect the hotel to pay for the missed flight or day's outing on the bus. The concierge had to be precise in taking breakfast orders, and telephone messages. There was no room for errors: you had to be perfect, the hotel had to be perfect.

Apart from his normal job in the reception hall – the paperwork of taking in the client's passports details, registering them on the police forms and on the hotel's computer – the porter had to do other things. When clients arrived with their luggage, he had to offer to carry the bags up the sixty steps to their room; sometimes the bags were light and easy, at other times they were heavy and back-breaking. Some people carry so much weight with them on their holiday; they bring a whole wardrobe. Unfortunately the hotel did not have a trolley, so all luggage was taken to the rooms by lifting and carrying it. It was possible to have a heart attack, because by the time the porter reached the sixtieth step with a weighty bag, he was out of breath and his heart was pounding like mad; sometimes he could feel it pounding in his throat. After depositing the luggage in the client's room, often without even getting a tip, he would have to rush down the sixty steps and take up his position behind the reception desk, now being visibly sweaty for all other hotel clients to see.

He had to be a one-man band. He had to have muscles too; he had to be fit and have a healthy heart.

The hotel laundry was halfway up the sixty steps. It was a big room containing all the facilities of a laundry, with an iron and a table, cupboards with clean sheets, etc. Three times a week the day staff would fill about thirty big sacks with dirty sheets. It was up to Luca to bring these heavy sacks down to street level, near the entrance of the hotel, so that the sacks could be collected by a van that took them away for washing.

The sacks were so heavy. At night it was difficult to see the external steps and path in the garden, lit sometimes only by the moonlight. The porter had to be quiet, too, so as not to wake the clients. He would drag the heavy sacks to the edge of the small terrace, and then with one hand gave the sack a heave, a lift and a push at the same time, as if he was helping the sack to take off with its own weight; this way he could throw the sacks down to the lower terrace, then down to the next terrace till he had them all stacked near the hotel drive. It was the easiest way to get the sacks down, but the management expected the porter to carry the bags by lifting and carrying, without dragging and throwing. The porter's method used up less energy and less effort, but it did not prevent him from tearing the tendon in his finger. His bent finger had to be strapped in a straight plastic cast for forty days, and it looked rather funny going round with one finger bandaged up like that and stuck in a straight and rigid strap! The last time the porter had had a bandage on an extremity was when he was very young, when he had stuck a thumb in a live light socket.

This had taken place in the back workroom of a small town shop. His tailor parents had been concentrating on the manufacture of the suit. To take advantage of the light coming from outside, they both sat near the front shop window. His father had one part of the garment and his mother the other, both of them concentrating and working with their hands, with their nimble fingers, with their needle and thread, working laboriously, with maximum concentration, with speed, in order to finish the hand made suit on time. The client must be satisfied. The porter's father always had to work to tight deadlines, so he had no time to go for walks, or to do any kind of exercise. He only had time for sewing and smoking his cigarettes in a hectic way.

The suit always had to be ready for the wedding or the funeral, for whatever occasion.

That day, whilst his parents were working, the dreamy porter who was about four years old at the time, was sitting at his father's huge tailoring table, playing with clothes brushes, imagining that they were cars and busses.

Above and beside the table in a dark corner was an old fashioned, down-facing U-shaped wall lamp, without the lampshade and light bulb. It seemed old and unused and appeared harmless, as if it was just an old museum piece, or just a big u shaped clothes hanger screwed to the wall above the worktable.

The child stopped playing with his clothes brushes, and, ignorant as to what was screwed to the wall, started to touch the wall lamp. At first the lamp frame metal felt cold and harmless, but his fingers kept on touching, exploring, from the top end of the light holder to the bottom end, which had the open empty socket. . His fingers slowly touched as if he had discovered a new toy. His fingers touched the cold

Rome

smooth metal, the empty socket seemed rather thrilling to the child. What was the opening? Why was the hole there? What were the two metallic contacts inside the opening? The child could not resist, his thumb had to explore, had to feel those contacts. In the dark corner of the room, sitting on a tall stool at the side of the worktable, the child moved his explorative thumb into the socket, and those old shiny but faded contacts seemed inviting too. He had to touch. Indeed he did. On contact, the child felt a surge of marching ants. The marching ants felt as if they had sharp needles as legs. From the tip of the thumb, the sensation seemed to surge slowly along his hand and up his arm. At first it felt like ants, but then the thumb felt as if the tip was being burnt, as if it was being grinded by sandpaper, as if microscopic wall drills were boring tiny holes into his thumb, grinding and eating the flesh away right down to the bone.

The sensation slowly amplified. The burning, surging sensation slowly penetrated his arm then his whole body. Before he could scream, he was already cemented to the electric light socket, bonded, and left literally hanging off the wall. His feet were no longer on the stool. His bonded thumb was all that was holding him up. He was hanging and being electrocuted.

The burning, stinging, vibrating electricity was crossing his whole body. The child felt the power, the surge; the voltage was running through him. It was frightening, terrifying.

The child looked up at his trapped thumb with terror. He felt as if he was being devoured from within by an invisible extraterrestrial entity. The voltage got stronger. His whole body was vibrating, slowly at first, then violently. To the child it seemed to happen in slow motion, but it was, in reality, instantaneous. A scream ultimately came. A scream: a violent, screeching scream.

Suddenly his parents looked round and in astonishment they saw their son hanging, hanging by his thumb hooked to an old light socket. The child's father reacted immediately. He instantaneously realized what was happening and without hesitating rushed across the workroom, in about five long-jump paces, to his son, and, with both strong determined hands and arms, with all his might, tore his son away from the socket. Two physically strong arms were needed to detach the child from the powerful electric grasp. The father had violently separated his son from certain death.

Luca was still lying on the bed, still unable to fall asleep. It was probably the excitement of being in new surroundings. Every time he changed beds, or slept somewhere new, he could never sleep… or was it the coffee? Perhaps he had drunk too many espressos that day. Now that he wanted to sleep he could not. Antonio in the other room was fast asleep, but his girlfriend was still at work.

The porter thought he should stop drinking coffee. He drank too much, especially when he was working every night; too much caffeine in the blood, he thought. Every night he would drink a strong cup of tea before going to work. He found that tea kept him awake for a few hours. Many times it prevented him from crashing his car when driving to work. Many a time his eyes were heavy, many a time his tiredness was so great that he had actually fallen asleep at the wheel. It was fortunate that the sleep only lasted a few seconds; he'd wake up just as the car started to go off the road. Shortly before arriving at work he would buy himself a coffee in a nearby bar. At work, friends from the restaurant next door would offer him a coffee. Later, at about eleven o'clock, he would go up into the hotel kitchen, switch on the espresso machine, and make himself another espresso, so by midnight he had already taken a lot of caffeine. Sometimes he would have a Coca-Cola to stimulate him even further. He needed all these drinks to keep him awake, as he slept poorly during the day.

The porter then thought back even further in time; he remembered the time he had drunk an ice-cold espresso when he was on holiday in Sicily. After drinking the liquid he'd felt dreadful, and had spent the next month in bed with jaundice and some kind of digestive disorder. He then promised himself never to drink ice-cold drinks again. Today, he wondered if excessive coffee drinking caused high blood pressure; it probably did.

The porter started to think about his health. He wondered how long he could keep on working nights. For how long would his body be able to sustain the change in the sleep-wake rhythm? It really was a problem trying to get to sleep every morning, and a problem every night trying to stay awake; he was continuously fighting his body's physiological needs.

Was he going to have a heart attack? He very much hoped not. He didn't like hospitals; he didn't want to spend more time in a hospital bed, as he had done many years ago.

He could still remember lying down on a trolley in the hospital operating theatre covered with a green overall. He was staring at the ceiling and had an oxygen mask over his face. The nurses, anaesthetists and doctors around him had their green masks on. One of them was holding his left hand, slowly injecting the anaesthetic into the patient's vein.

Luca remembered breathing the strange smelling oxygen from the mask, and recalled trying to distract himself by making himself count backwards and simultaneously thinking of a pleasant seaside scenery. Soon he became conscious that at any moment he would fall asleep unwillingly and unnaturally, with the possibility of never waking up. Although he was weak and drowsy, he was well aware that the anaesthetic was on its way to his brain, through the vein, like a train racing through a tunnel.

He waited, waited and waited. Those moments seemed interminable, but when the train arrived, his vision quickly darkened, as if in a dark tunnel. Like a dark, heavy black buzzing curtain that seemed to noisily, boldly, shift its way into his head, across his eyes like a blanket of black tar, sealing his sight from the outside world. The porter was aware of this transition; the moments the blackout occurred. He saw it all in his mind, he was aware of it. But once the curtain hit the bottom of his screen, he was away.

He could remember waking up whilst still being

operated on in the operating theatre. His hands were tied together and he was lying on one side. Luca was immobilised, paralysed by the anaesthetic; he could not have moved a finger even if he'd tried with all his might. He could not open his eyes, so he couldn't see anything, only the black screen of his closed eyelids. He could not see, but he could hear the surgeons talking; their words were not clear, they were muffled and echoing. He could hear them but didn't know what they were saying. All Luca wanted to do was communicate with them, to signal to them that he was awake, he wanted to warn them that he was conscious and that he could feel all that was being done to him, he could therefore feel the pain; feel the scalpel cut, if they were about to cut him.

The porter tried desperately to move his forefinger; he tried with all his strength, but to no avail; he felt a long rod-like tool being inserted into his back; it scraped the inside of his ribcage. It was excruciating pain, but Luca could not scream; not out loud, anyhow, he could only scream in his mind, and nobody could hear him. Fortunately, the surgeons were terminating the operation on his lung. He felt a big slap on his back, which really hurt.

It was soon all over; he could feel himself being accompanied to the intensive care ward, the operation was over, but there followed weeks of pain and nursing care before he could even leave the hospital.

The porter lay there and thought what a bad time that had been; he would definitely not like to spend any more time in a hospital. He still remembered the time before the operation when he came so close to death. He remembered lying on a trolley, waiting to be diagnosed. He was flat on his back, his breathing was laboured, each inhalation was so short, and getting shorter all the time, he really thought his days were numbered. The nurse beside him was calmly taking down his personal details with a pen on a notepad.

The weeks that followed were weeks of pain. He was suffering from a collapsed lung, and a plastic tube was inserted into the ribcage, from the ribcage to a bell jar; this jar always had to be below chest level. It was half-filled with water.

To insert the tube, the doctors and nurses pulled the curtain around the patient's bed. They gathered around, put on their masks and peered down at the breathless, suffocating Luca who was flat on his back. All five of them looked like five dentists looking down the patient's throat. The senior doctor said to Luca, 'Don't worry, keep calm. We will now relieve you of the pain and the tight sensation in your chest.'

The nearby nurse handed the senior doctor what looked at first like a knitting needle, but on closer examination, was a long metallic rod, with a sharp end.

'Be calm, you won't feel anything,' said the physician. He looked at Luca in the eyes, then positioned the sharp end of the rod on Luca's exposed chest, in between two ribs near the top end of the rib cage. 'You will feel a bit of pressure, that's all,' he said. He positioned himself over Luca, holding the metallic rod-like instrument vertically, and grasped it firmly with both his clenched fists. The doctor started to push the rod, lightly at first, then gradually with a little more force. A little blood could be seen squirting away from the drilling point.

'Don't worry, it's only a little blood," said the reassuring medic. Luca could feel no pain, but he did feel the rod pressure mounting between his ribs, over his air-filled chest. The arrow-type rod did not go in so easily. The doctor added more pressure; he positioned himself better over the patient, almost leaning on top of him; doing so, he was able to have a better grip and to add more weight behind the rod. The doctor pushed and pushed until the sharp end of the rod managed to squeeze in between the tight ribs and perforate the chest cavity. When the final push came after a sudden jolt, the other medical staff and nurses let off a tension-releasing cheer. Without wasting any time, they inserted a transparent plastic tube into the new hole, into the punctured ribcage.

'Cough, cough, cough now,' someone said. Luca forced a cough and suddenly the mounting pressure in his chest was relieved, like a dam suddenly breached. He could breath a little, and it suddenly felt like life was flowing back into him.

Every time Luca coughed, a green, frothy liquid came out of his chest into the tube, and then air bubbles could be seen in the bell jar. He had to have this jar with him day and night; he could not be separated from it. Whenever the nurses had to take him to have an X-ray taken in another part of the hospital, the bell jar had to follow him; they sat him on a wheelchair and put the jar between his legs. After the operation, he couldn't move very far, and still couldn't breathe normally; he was out of breath with every small movement.

He was confined to bed and the chair for weeks. Luca could not sleep when he was in hospital. The pain from his surgical wounds kept him awake all night, for many nights. He thought it was hell, and could never have imagined a worse situation. At night he couldn't move, nor during the day, because he had so many tubes attached to him: tubes to his chest, to his side and tubes to his arm and wrist. He could not move because he was tied down, and he was getting really sore from sitting in the same position all the time. Occasionally the night nurse moved him, and gave him painkillers; he was totally reliant on the nurse, but the pain of the wounds would not ease for hours. It was torture, so, night after night, he was kept awake. They seemed interminable nights, it was like a nightmare, also because there were other patients who were in agony, other patients in the ten-bed ward who were agonising, moaning and groaning and calling out for the nurse – for something, for a drink, or for another painkiller. Those nights were really a torment; they seemed to dwarf the nights he would work in the hotel many years later.

Recovering from the operation was a long and slow process. Luca could not eat much, so his weight dropped. When he tried to walk he swayed and needed help and support, and he had lost not only a lot of blood, but a lot of strength too.

Those days were long gone, the porter thought. That had been a real battle for survival – the battle to keep on living.

The porter looked around the room; he still had the table lamp on next to his bed, his mobile phone was still on but only occasionally did it have a signal. He checked to see if he had received any messages; he had voice messages from his mother, and text messages from Ireland, from his old friend whom he was going to visit. His mother, in her seventies, had left a message saying she was concerned that he hadn't phoned her for a while; his old friend, too, had left a message asking him if he was all right. The porter, too, was asking himself 'Am I all right?' He asked himself what he was doing going on a long train journey. Was it more than just a journey? Was it an escape? Was it a search for something?

The porter was always in search of something, always escaping. He was always in search of himself, he was like one man, split into two separate identical beings, but with halved physical, mental and moral strength. He was a man cut in two, one being the angel, the other the devil. Until Luca could find unity, he would be weak in every aspect. He would always be an indecisive and insecure man. He felt as if his mind had many persons, many bosses, none of whom could agree on anything, like a board meeting where managers have different opinions, all of them perfect and correct, but no one resolution can be passed. Like the saying, 'Too many cooks spoil the broth', he had too many leaders in his mind, but no chairman to come up with the final answer. He had a parliament in his head that could not reach a final vote on anything. It was his nightmare; it was like having a prisoner's ball and chain attached to his ankle, which impeded his movement. It impeded him from being the person he wanted to be. He felt as if his own self constantly held him back.

Milan

It was nearly dawn and almost time to make his departure from Antonio's flat. His next stop would be Milan, the city where he had spent three years of his life; it was a good job that he was only passing through, as the metropolis had also given him some unpleasant memories.

Luca got up, looked out of the window at all the apartment terraces, most of them covered with big vases and plants; it was an elegant neighbourhood. Antonio got up and prepared an espresso. The porter still could not believe the disorder that the kitchen was in. They both drank their small, black, strong espressos; and then they walked out on to the balcony to have a look outside. Little was said, so after only one hour, the porter made his way with his luggage and opened the apartment door. He pressed a button and called the lift, which promptly arrived. They said their goodbyes, and as the lift arrived at their floor and opened its doors, the porter entered the lift and left.

He made his way down on the lift, out of the building and down the road to the entrance of the underground. There were still hardly any people rushing to work, so he found it quite easy to get on the tube and make his way to the central railway station. Here, he waited only half an hour before getting on the train bound for Milan. It was train with no compartments, it looked more like the inside of a plane or a

Milan

very long coach, and it was full of people going to work. The train soon left the station and gathered speed, and as it travelled through the city he could see several Roman monuments: the Coliseum and the long aqueduct. Soon the train ventured into the misty Roman countryside.

It was strange to see so many people all at once; there was a mixture of races, not just Romans, all going in the direction of Milan, the city of work, design, and fashion. The journey from Rome to the second city of Italy would take six to seven hours, so it gave the porter more time to contemplate and to reflect.

He was on his way back to the big industrial metropolis, the city he lived in for three years. He suddenly remembered the first night he had spent in the tiny flat, in the company of his mother. His first night in Italy started off with a bang, a big explosive display. Lying on his hard bed, in the semi-dark apartment, he could see a light coming into the room, of which seemed to be reflections of a fire. He looked out of the window, and not far away he could see a car in flames. The fire was lighting up the neighbourhood; the reflection of the flames could be seen on all the walls of all the high-rise flats that were in the block. Was it the Mafia? Was it some criminal with a grudge against the car owner? Being his first night in Milan, it seemed like a warning from the supernatural telling him, 'Welcome to hell!'

The porter remembered having left England only a few hours previously. He had got on a plane – had done what he hated and feared. He had left his safe haven to risk a new adventure in the big Italian city,

Milan

and he had not been pleased with his first impressions. Driving from the airport to his new one-roomed apartment, he could see a row of prostitutes standing along the roundabout of a major road leading into the city centre, and along the way, all the side streets were jammed with parked cars. Everything seemed so overcrowded and congested, even if the new city was much bigger than the city he had left a few hours ago. So with the sight of tall prostitutes, half-naked on the street, and the sight of the car that had been set on fire by vandals in the neighbourhood, the young man was not at all glad that he had come, that he had stepped on the aeroplane to come to Milan. In fact, all he wanted to do was go back straight away.

He felt uncomfortable in his new surroundings. The flat was on the seventh floor, and it was small. It had one bedroom, which was also a living room. There was a small kitchen and a small bathroom, it was a smaller than average apartment. There were two beds, a leather sofa, and an old dressing table. Next to the dressing table was a small black and white TV, which barely worked. The view from the flat was quite good; one could see other, similar flats everywhere. In the extreme distance one could see the Alps, the chain of mountains that divides Italy from France.

Apart from the furniture, the flat was in excellent condition; but it felt, to say the least, like a prison cell. He was used to having bigger rooms and more space.

The porter relaxed on the train. He stretched his legs out and kept on looking out of the window. The fog and mist had lifted outside, so now he could see the beautiful countryside.

His thoughts went back to the Milan flat. He could not understand why he had spent three years in the city and in that particular hole. What kept him there, he didn't exactly know. It took him three years to recognise that the novelty of the new city had worn off, that he now desperately wanted to get away from the place. He could not get used to the size of the city, the chaotic traffic, the constant need to use the underground and buses to get from A to B. After squeezing into the underground train where the commuters were packed together like salted sardines in a can, he had to push like mad to get out at the right underground station. Bodies were squashed together, and you were aware of everything. Sometimes it was pleasant to lean against a nice blonde, sometimes a disaster to rub up against a malodorous, obese old man. The porter felt trapped and claustrophobic wherever he went. There were so many people everywhere, not only on the underground but also up on the streets, people running around in different directions, all in a mad hurry; he could see faces of different types, strange faces. He would go back to his miserable flat feeling exhausted and dizzy. His feet would ache from the amount of walking he had done, and he often walked without any fixed direction, so he was disorientated like a mouse in a maze. He felt dizzy, like a man on a children's roundabout spinning around at high speeds. He was not ill but he was getting there. After his daily runaround in the metropolis, he went home and felt trapped in a cage. The lift to the seventh floor apartment was only big enough for two or three people, adding to the claustrophobic feeling of being caged. At times it was like a bad dream. If one wanted to go out and socialise at night, there would be nowhere to go, and not having a car he would be forced to watch the old black and white TV, which had a bad picture. At the time it felt like a very unfortunate situation.

When he wasn't out in the city getting lost among the crowd, he was in the flat; he would spend days there without going out, trapped there, looking out of the window, watching the world get up in the morning to go to work, and watching the world come home at night. In between he would spend hours in silence, listening to the clock ticking away. Listening for any little noise that would come from the flat next door, listening to the sound of the lift going up and down, and its doors opening and closing. He would spend interminable hours shut away in the room, alone, not knowing what to do, not noticing the relentless passage of time. He was not a prisoner, but he felt like one, as if an invisible jail surrounded him.

The train was speeding away towards Milan, the city of work, of fashion. He just could not believe he had spent so much time there, wasted time. Where did his mind go? Why did he allow so much time to elapse? Was he in dream world? Was his head buried in the sand? Was he momentarily on another planet, out of this world? At the time he had sometimes wondered if he was in fact an alien, an alien that departs the body to go wandering elsewhere in the form of an invisible phantom...

The fact that he had been unemployed had not helped his self-esteem. The fact that he had nothing to do all day left him time – too much time – to think. It was like being a football player left on the bench on the sideline in a football match. He was like a player momentarily out of action.

He would watch TV for some of the time, then when he got tired and fed up he would make himself a cup of coffee. He would give himself a break from the boredom by digging his teeth into a biscuit; at least the sugar content would give his bored mind something to get the brain cells to vibrate again. He thought how working people often longed for some time off to just sit and relax and do nothing, to sit alone in a room to contemplate. Some people might need that and love it, but here was a man going mad, not having anyone to talk to, alone but for his own thoughts.

A day stuck in a room alone seemed interminable. Reading a book sometimes helped, but not for long; he would soon have another tea or coffee with biscuits. He would long for the clock to chime at midday, so at least he would then have something to do, to prepare lunch. He would be able to use his imagination, his creativity to invent something new, create a new dish for his lunch. He would go into the kitchen and cook something for himself and that took up some time; it distracted him from the empty void of that day. His cooking was usually very simple, but sometimes he would try something new and unusual. He enjoyed cooking, and enjoyed eating, and every day he got into the habit of including spaghetti with all his newly created dishes.

In time, his stomach slowly but surely began to get bigger and bigger. The belt around his waist needed to be adjusted. Every day he would get the bowl of cooked spaghetti, put it on the table and then dig his fork into the pasta, look at the spaghetti and say, 'Spaghetti, I am now going to kill you'; then he would turn the spaghetti on and around the fork and shove it all into his mouth. The following ten to fifteen minutes would give him great gratification, and would distract him from his gloom and mental disorientation.

Every morning and every night, however, he would stand in front of the mirror to look at himself, to look at his profile and to daily observe the increasing size of his abdomen.

Eventually he'd found a job in a small company. Every day he would commute to and from his employment. His employer was a bearded, blue-eyed man. He had a cold, penetrating stare, enough to freeze your spinal cord. He was a quiet man who expected work to be done with professional excellence, even by his newest employees. The porter worked there for a few months and never really enjoyed his work or his workplace. He didn't get on with the employer, and as a result he left the job gladly. He felt as if he was being used, and clearly felt he was underpaid.

He soon found work in another small company, run by a German husband and wife. There, too, he found his employers to be strange people. One morning when he went to work, the husband opened the apartment door. The porter was shocked to see the man topless, and his whole chest covered in red scratches. His wife was a big, big woman. He was tall and very thin; together they looked like Laurel and Hardy. What they had been up to, the porter didn't know, but it stirred his imagination. Did they have a fight, or were they just having fun? What also made it strange to work in that apartment was the fact that the porter had to listen to the fat woman sing opera music all day. She was a former opera singer. The porter was not keen on that type of music. He didn't like opera, and needless to say he didn't like that high-pitched voice hollering all day long. The ex-singer would walk down the corridor singing, would go to the bathroom singing, and would have lunch and tea and supper singing to her heart's content. So it all seemed strange. The place, his employers, the surroundings and the sounds, were not his scene.

One good thing about being in Milan was the fact he could visit the museums, churches, art galleries, monuments, squares, and shopping centres. He was a perennial tourist, but in the back of his mind there was a dark corner that he wanted to illuminate. He was in an enduring state of obscurity, which made all his sightseeing tours surreal. He remembered visiting the Leonardo da Vinci Museum, with all its technical and scientific inventions. Models of war and flying machines could be admired there, together with his paintings and drawings. The porter thought back to the days when he had studied the great painter and inventor for his college thesis, the days when the mere observation of Leonardo's drawings of anatomy started a very dark and depressing phase.

Luca thought back to Leonardo's drawings; he recalled how those illustrations of anatomy – of human anatomy – had made him literally ill. The mere sight of the internal parts of the body, the heart, the lungs, the intestines, had sparked off a deep fear of death. Studying the anatomy had suddenly made the porter realise that we are not immortal. The reality of life and death had dawned on him: life was real, and death was real and inevitable.

He suddenly realised that he had a physical body that was very fragile. He became so afraid that he could not go to sleep at night for fear of not waking up any more. In his bed at night he would stay awake, and as soon as he realised he was falling asleep he would wake himself up with fear. He felt as if falling asleep meant the curtains were coming down on his life. If he fell asleep his existence would cease. For weeks he could not close his eyes and fall asleep without this terrible anxiety; every little twitch in his head was to him an imminent brain haemorrhage. A little pain on his chest was an imminent heart attack. He had thought heart attacks were reserved for older people, not for the young. When friends would mention the death of a young twenty-year-old, he would go into a deep depression, and his fears would get bigger and bigger. Our lives, our existence, can't depend on a fleshy heart, he thought. We can't be that fragile, surely!

All these fears had caused Luca great distress, so much so that he began to feel awful. The more he thought about it the more his fears grew. Every little pain, twitch or ache was a major concern for him. He started to hear and feel a clicking tick in his chest, and that made him terrified. He thought he was about to die.

Luca had gone to Milan, to one of the biggest hospitals and had a check-up. The specialists listened to his chest, placed several monitor pads on his torso and took readings. The sight of all these doctors around him made his heartbeat speed up, and he became more and more anxious. His blood pressure readings shot up to a very high level. The doctors were concerned but could not find anything wrong with him. One young inexperienced doctor, looking at the blood pressure results, told him, 'You will be a corpse at the age of thirty, at this rate, if you continue to be so anxious.'

At this point Luca thought even further back in time to when he was just thirteen. Quick images flashed by in his mind of when his father died suddenly of a heart attack. He remembered lying in bed and hearing his father run down the corridor, his feet thudding, in a desperate need to get to the bathroom, as he was feeling unwell... then, moments later, running quickly back to the bedroom, still in a desperate rush to get there. His father was probably desperately trying to run away from the pain that his heart was giving him. The porter remembered hearing his father's last desperate gasps for air; his demands to have the window open to let the air in. 'Open the window! Open, open, I can't breathe! Let some air in; open, open the window!'

Then Luca had heard a last, heavy *thump*. There followed screams of panic and desperation; his mother had been alarmed and horrified at the unpleasant incident. Luca remembered getting out of bed, shivering with fright and cold as it was a chilly, bitter February night. He ran to his parent's bedroom and saw his father sitting on the floor, at the side of the bed, with his back up against it. The window was wide open, but his mother was not there, she was in another room, telephoning for medical assistance.

The young adolescent could tell that there was nothing to be done; his father's head was slumped down over his chest, eyes already closed. He remembered approaching his father and trying to revive him in his own way, by moving his father's head and trying to free the air passage, which seemed blocked. He tried moving his arms, which were flaccid, but still warm. He was warm all over, he looked as if he was sleeping, but he would not respond to anything, not even to slaps on the face or loud calls. Perhaps he had just fainted, or become momentarily unconscious, the young boy thought; perhaps there was a chance to revive him... But eventually he realised that there was nothing he could do.

He remembered the arrival of the ambulance and police, the doctor and his father's best friend, and he also remembered the priest. He remembered being set aside in another room with his mother, who was crying out of desperation, embracing him and his sister. He remembered the image of his dead father on the bed, covered from head to foot with a bed sheet, lying there motionless. He remembered the cold feeling that came over him: the chilling thought that there had been a death in that bedroom, that the spirit had left the body, left a coldness in the bedroom. He also remembered the two men who took his father away, his father wrapped in a white cloth hauled down the steps and out into the men's black transport van. They did not use a stretcher, but heaved him as if he was an old rolled up carpet, wrapped up like an Egyptian mummy.

Milan

The train had stopped and started at different stations and Milan was now only a couple of hours away. While the porter was thinking back in time, he was still contemplating and looking at the scenery outside the window of the train. The countryside was now more flat and spacious, compared to the tight, mountainous regions of the south. Could the surroundings have an effect on people's minds and mentality, he thought, in the same way that different climates have a different effect on people's skin and physical appearance? How fortunate the people of the north of Italy were! They had so much space. Wide open flat fields – but not quite as green as Ireland, the country he was going to.

The porter thought of all the people from the south who had migrated to the north to find work. People having to leave home, leaving their families behind in order to search for a better future. In former days, at the beginning of the twentieth century, it was easier to find work in other parts of the world, such as in America, Australia and Germany, but today it wasn't easy for anybody to find work anywhere. The changing times meant you had to be the best, the competition meant you needed good qualifications; you had to keep up with constant technological changes, you needed to keep renewing the level or standard of your qualifications, because the ones you already had would become obsolete, and before you got that interview you had to write a perfect curriculum vitae. Then there were the replies, mostly negative ones, to tell you 'Sorry, on this occasion you have not been successful.'

People in the past found it difficult to survive, so too do the people of today find it difficult, a constant battle to be fought. The porter thought, Wouldn't it have been better to live in the Stone Age? Then, all you needed was food, clothing heat and shelter obtainable in less academic and modern ways. Yes, perhaps that's what's needed, a time machine to go back and live a simpler life at a slower pace.

If you do work today, you are stressed; you live like a clock, like a robot to keep a certain standard of living. You become a machine, you have no time to unwind; you are constantly on the move, to keep up with the so-called 'rat race'. You are in a constant, continuous fight to keep your head above water. Milan was one of the many cities to experience and live in, like other big cities in the world, if you wanted a better feel of the rat race.

The railway station in Milan seemed old in comparison to Rome's modern station. But there he was in Milan, halfway to Ireland. He decided to eat another sandwich, which was tucked away in his sports bag. He found an empty bench and sat himself down. The bread and cheese *panino* made in Sicily was a little dry by now, but it still seemed fit for human consumption. There were pigeons all around him waiting for a bit of bread to fall on the floor; he still had his bottle of mineral water, a banana and an apple. He was quite hungry. He had an hour before the next train left for Paris, but he wasted no time and ate.

Paris

Luca soon found his place on the Paris train. It was a very comfortable, modern train; the quality seemed to be getting better the further north one went. The train from Sicily to Rome had been old; the seats worn, dilapidated and damaged. From Rome to Milan, the situation had been a little better, the train more up-to-date and clean. But the train from Milan to Paris seemed by far the best, with comfortable, clean seats and more space, and a modern design. Luca placed his luggage in the compartment provided and moved to his reserved seat near the wide window. He took his jacket off and sat down, looking all around him to take in the view of his new home for the forthcoming hours. No reserved sleeping carriages or flip-down beds this time, only seats. It was only four o'clock in the afternoon. He calculated that the train would arrive in Paris about midnight, so a bed wasn't really necessary.

The messages on his mobile were now becoming rare from his mother in Sicily; they were becoming a little more frequent from his friend in Ireland. The battery in his phone only had a third of the power left, so he had to use it in moderation. He had nowhere to recharge his mobile; no sockets were available on this train. It wasn't like the first class train he'd travelled on the year before, which not only provided the sockets for plugs but also a small bathroom and shower

Paris

cubicle. You were even given *spumante* and peanuts at the beginning of the journey, and a full breakfast in the morning with a newspaper to read.

So the porter sat there, looking out on to the platform where other travellers were still running around trying to find the carriage that contained their reserved seats. His glance out of the window slowly turned into a gaze, then into a fixed stare, then into a daydreaming condition. He realised that soon he would be meeting up with the woman he had been receiving messages from since he started his journey in Sicily.

Who was this woman he was going to meet in Paris? Well, he knew her very well. She was a very old friend who he'd first met many years ago. They'd both been in their teens when they'd first encountered each other: he'd been nineteen and she, fifteen. They were now much older, in fact, middle-aged, and about to meet up in Paris. Luca was going on a holiday, but it was an unusual holiday. Perhaps that's what made his journey a journey of unease, because he was taking a trip down memory lane, to the past, to when they were both young and living in England – not like today, with one living in Sicily and the other living in Ireland.

Luca was now at the halfway stage; he was on the train destined for Paris. He was still inside Italy, the country he had got used to living in, with its different climate and culture. He was about to leave, as it seemed to him, one planet in order to visit another. It felt very much like a rocket launch, and the porter felt he was a space traveller. The fear of leaving this warm country, with its warm blue skies, its hot summers, its sandy beaches populated with tourists, was getting

Paris

greater and greater. He was taking off, leaving this remarkable planet; he was leaving and going northwards beyond the atmosphere of the Alps, north to the cold climates of France, England and Ireland. He wondered if he could get used to the rain and cold again. Could he get used to this wintry environment after so many years spent in the sunny south? On the train, there were now fewer Sicilians and Italians. Instead, there were now mostly French and English-speaking travellers. These passengers with their paler skins were already giving the porter an uncomfortable sensation. Should he get off the train and abort the mission? Should he stay in Milan a few days, visit his uncle and old friends, then make a U-turn and go back to Sicily? Or should he continue with the journey?

He was very tempted to get off the train. Could he withstand any more hours listening to the train's incessant, repetitive rattle and track noise? Maybe he'd had enough... The time for deciding what to do quickly ran out. Within minutes the train was slowly moving out of Milan Station. He was on his way north. It was too late; fate or destiny had put him there and now he could only go along with it. He wasn't going to jump off the train, so he decided to sit back and continue with the trip, accepting his fate.

The train gathered pace, and within half an hour the locomotive and convoy of carriages, the extremely long terrestrial space rocket, was speeding out into the countryside, racing towards the French and Italian Alps. It was, for the hotel porter, like taking off on a space mission and leaving the earth's atmosphere.

Paris was getting closer every second, and Luca kept

looking out of the window, looking at the countryside, at all the roads and houses that could be seen dotted around. He looked out at the plain flat open fields, a sharp contrast to the harsh hills and mountains of Sicily. It felt very much like an escape, an escape from a prison camp, an escape from the nights of work in the hotel, an escape from his colleagues, his menacing superiors, an escape from the claustrophobic hills and mountains of Sicily, from the narrow streets, from the incessant noise of the neighbour's drills and hammers banging on the walls. For the porter, the journey carried a mixture of apprehension and liberation, a feeling of wanting to go, and not wanting to go on this holiday. He was running away from a bad dream of the present, running towards the past, to the known past, but an uncertain future.

Hour after hour, Paris was getting closer. An Indian man sat in the seat next to him. He was young, but strangely he had two fingers stuck together, actually fused together in one skin. He, too, was going to Paris.

It was not long before the train started to go through tunnels, long tunnels. It was going through the Alps, and Luca thought that that was the end of the warm weather, the end of the sunshine.

Between the tunnels, Luca could look at the dominating mountains. Some were higher than others; most were sharp and rugged like pyramids, covered in a blanket of white snow, encompassed by clouds. One in particular stood out amongst the others, the king of the Alps, Mount Blanc, with its peak reaching high, up towards the heavens. For a split second Luca thought of skiing disasters, of avalanches, and also of his

Paris

childhood memories of crossing the snow-laden alps in his parents' car, in the days before tunnels were built, driving through dangerous meandering, sometimes slippery, foggy and snow-covered roads, frequently behind or in front of long heavy goods lorries. He remembered the time he had nearly slipped down a crevice, as he was about to take a panoramic photograph of the rugged mountains. The thought of the near fall made him think of the First World War, of the Italian soldiers who had climbed the steep jagged mountains of the eastern Alps, to fight the Austrians, to defend the Italian borders. His thoughts then went on to one particular soldier, to his grandfather, who had been shot in the eye. The bullet hit the eye at such an angle that it had emerged through the cheek of the face and continued its trajectory through the shoulder, to emerge out of the soldier's back. The eye was completely destroyed, but fortunately the bullet missed any other organs or arteries. Miraculously that day, Lucas's grandfather's life was spared.

Luca then had a momentary mental picture of Hannibal and his barbarian army of warriors with their enormous elephants crossing the mountain passageways between the peaks, with the intent of invading and destroying the Roman Empire many centuries ago.

At the exit of the longest and final tunnel, Luca could see snow here and there; the temperature was lower, freezing. It was clear that the train was in France. It had crossed the border between Italy and France and none of the passengers noticed the crossing. The train stopped and started several times, but it soon picked up speed. Now the sun was definitely gone, instead of blue

Paris

skies above there were only grey clouds. Further into the journey, the porter could see and hear rain whipping against the train windows. It was a long time since he'd seen rain and he could not make up his mind if he liked it or not. It was depressing to look at, but at the same time it was a refreshing change.

He was getting closer to Paris, and it was daylight. Luca had plenty of time to stare out of the window and contemplate. The Indian man sitting next to him spoke occasionally, between studying his verbs and looking at his book. He was on his way to the French capital too. Luca spoke when spoken to, but in general kept to himself, kept quiet. After a while it was clear to the Indian that Luca didn't want to be disturbed.

Being a quiet man, Luca went through life, experiencing it in a solitary way. He generally didn't like to talk and thought he wasn't good at it. In a group or crowd he would go about quiet and inhibited, wouldn't speak, and absolutely hated being the centre of attention. He was a reserved man. Family and close friends would time and again say that he was too quiet, never talked, never uttered a word. The trend had started at a very young age, and continued to the present day. Luca liked working nights for this reason; he had a limited contact with people, and stayed on his own for most of the time whilst on duty. Some clients, the more friendly and outgoing extroverts would hang about in the foyer at the reception desk and engage the porter in long and lengthy conversations. Sometimes Luca enjoyed the company and the long discussions; sometimes he hated it and wished that the person or persons would go away.

Paris

He remembered one man, who was a Taormina resident. He was short and chubby but quite a good-looking chap. He would often come into the hotel at three in the morning to give Luca long accounts of his escapades with foreign female tourists. He would tell a long tedious story, then go into all the erotic details of his adventures with these uncomplicated women. At least he made it seem as if it was all true; he seemed to think of himself as an irresistible Casanova. The porter would often have to stand there and listen to his many true, or fictitious, adventures, and on some occasions Luca stood there literally falling asleep. The man, who had reddish hair, spent most of his days on the beach, chasing German or American women; or he would go deep sea diving to fish for his evening supper. He certainly didn't seem to have a job, not a steady one in any case. He probably helped out in some pizzeria in the town, but who could believe what he said or did was true? He was bluffing half the time. On his way to work, Luca would sometimes see him on the side of the road, hitch-hiking, trying to get a lift to town at the top of the hill. Then Luca would stop to give him a lift, but reluctantly, as the red-haired diver frequently carried a plastic bag full of freshly caught fish, which would invariably contaminate Luca's car with its fishy smell.

As soon as he go into the car, the man would often put his hand out to shake hands, but on most occasions Luca tried to avoid physical contact. Who knows where the man had been? What had he touched? Who had he been with? As soon as he sat in the car he started talking about his escapades. Not only would Luca give him a lift some evenings, when he had the bad luck to meet him on the side of the road, but would also have to talk with him till late in the night at the reception desk in the hotel foyer. The porter didn't have the audacity to be impolite and tell the man to go away. Although the visitor was a self-described Casanova, he seemed to be a vulgar man too, so Luca tolerated him, pretending to appear interested in his dirty stories to keep him happy.

His stories were quite unbelievable. He told tales of chatting up women and having sex with them in awkward places and times, often on the very first night, sometimes having sex with two or three women at the same time, in a group. He seemed so proud, showing off, telling the world he was a really virile, active male, a real Sicilian. He would go around the town stopping his friends and other acquaintances in the street to tell them the stories. The concierge was probably the last person to be put in the picture, in the early hours of the morning.

The red-haired man was the self-proclaimed chief woman-hunter and trapper. There were other men, too, in the town of Taormina, who thought they were God's gift to women. Luca frequently went for short walks in the central Corso Umberto before going to work. He would notice how some men would parade up and down the street incessantly, dressed in their best suits, sometimes alone, sometimes with a friend. They would walk as if they were on parade, as if they were on show. They would continuously look left, look right, look behind and in front to see if they could see any prey, any Nordic women to chase for the evening. They would look with eagle eyes to see if they had been noticed, to see if they were in the eyes or in the minds of some voluptuous blonde, looking for a hot Sicilian holiday adventure. It often takes just one glance from the *galletto*, (the rooster), to make a decisive hit on some prey. They know that many foreign women go there, not just for the sun, sea, ice cream, pasta and pizza, but also to try out the Sicilian male. So it was easy for them; it was just a matter of time to make a hit.

The quiet porter at times hated staying up half the night, keeping the hotel doors open, just to allow the red-haired man to tell his dirty stories. He would say, 'I put my hand on her breast... I put my hand between her thighs... she begged for more... I put it there and she loved it... she wants to see me again...' And so he went, on and on.

Sometimes Luca had pleasant encounters. He would meet interesting people, people from different social and economic backgrounds, people from different parts of the world, from far away China, Japan, and Australia, even from the island of Hawaii. Sometimes he would meet famous personalities, actors and singers.

On one occasion a very famous Italian singer walked in. She had just performed at the Greek theatre and was extremely tired. It was strange to see such a famous person in the flesh, usually seen on the TV; here she was, only a few feet away from Luca. She was extremely well known, but she was not so young any more. She came in the foyer in a hurry, never even made eye contact with the porter, then asked for her room keys. Luca needed to make her sign a hotel check-in form, but in his urgency and nervousness, he could not find the forms, which were usually under the reception desk. He put his hand on to the shelves, behind the desk, moving his hand around trying to find them the block of forms. The singer all of a sudden panicked, and started to lose her cool.

'What are you doing, what are you looking for?' she exclaimed 'Get on with it – I am tired, give me my keys!'

Luca thought that she reckoned he was reaching out for a gun or a similar weapon. She lost her nerve and patience with the porter, and got very angry. In the end, he showed her to her room without getting her to sign the check-in form. Luca was astonished at her nastiness, and from that moment on, every time he saw her singing on TV he thought what a vicious person she was, rather than being the perfect human being on the TV screen.

It was inevitable that Luca met many young women; they came to the hotel in twos or threes. Some were very attractive, some plain, and some were monstrous. There were many types, but on some occasions the porter lost his shyness and talked with the women. The concierge is usually the first Sicilian male that the travelling woman meets. He had to check them in, show them to their rooms, and advise them on where to go to eat for the evening. He was the first, so he had the first attempt at them.

Sometimes he would meet shy, quiet women like the Chinese or Japanese. They would always smile, be polite and courteous, while the porter would some-

Paris

times try to chat them up, often with long inquisitive questions about Japan or China. He would ask the usual predictable questions like, 'Where do you come from?' 'Where do you live?' 'What job do you do?' and so on. He would be kind and polite to them, but on many occasions it was all to no avail. By the time the Japanese walked to the restaurant, had their evening meal and had taken a stroll, they were taken or booked or held in reserve by the young Sicilian scavengers casually roaming the city street for prey.

That seemed to happen quite often. Beautiful and pretty women would get caught in the trap. Young Sicilian men and foreign women would find each other in the streets of Taormina. Luca would almost always be left empty-handed; he would often have to wait up for most of the night for the return of his new female guests. The young girls would leave the hotel, alone, on foot, and return late at night accompanied by a Sicilian male, driving a motorbike or Lambretta, or daddy's big automobile.

Luca was not always so unfortunate. Many women passed him by in the lobby, but only the single guests dared to stop and talk to him in the reception area. Some would stay for hours in front of the desk all evening, trying to keep a conversation going with the porter.

If they spoke English it was an advantage. Being able to communicate in the same language was very helpful, and it gave the women a sense of belonging.

Sometimes, Luca decided to go to work in his blue suit wearing his favourite red tie. He noticed that clients would smile at him more; they would be more generous and give him tips on their departure. It appears that the red tie made them feel better, happier. It also attracted certain women, who found men in smart dress, smart suits, to be appealing, just as some women are attracted to men in uniforms. Well, the suit was like a uniform. Luca remembered one particular woman who virtually threw herself at him, and eventually invited him to visit her in her home town, there in the island of Sicily itself. She was very eye-catching. She had long black hair and dark brown penetrating eyes, and a good figure.

He did visit her, but the place was too far away. He struggled to get there with his old Renault 5, which could have fallen to pieces at any moment. He did, however, notice that the magic of the red tie wore off. In his ordinary casual clothes without the neat-looking tie, he was not interesting any more. He did not excite the females as much, and eventually his brief friendship with the pretty Sicilian came to an end. The porter came to the strange conclusion that it was the tie, or the fact that he did not wear it outside the hotel in everyday life, that made the woman slowly lose interest in him. The tie really did have a mysterious effect on certain clients while he was wearing it. How strange... was it the colour red? The Sicilian girl had cooked him something special. In particular, he had enjoyed her creamy pesto ravioli.

After the luscious meal she had invited Luca into the quiet living room, sat him at a round table and offered to read his future. She had taken Luca's hands into hers, looked at his palms attentively, studied the creases and lines, and after a slow increase of mystic atmosphere she had stared deep into his eyes with her own magical dark eyes and said in a soft voice, 'You will go on a journey, far, far away. You will meet with someone from the past.' After the brief sitting the seductive woman had prepared and typed out on paper a detailed study of Lucas' full astrological chart and then had given it to him before he had left.

Luca worked nights not just because he accidentally fell into the job, but also because he preferred to be out of his house in the evenings and at night. His home village was so quiet and uneventful; it did not offer any form of entertainment. The local people just did not have the habit of going out at night, so during the winter the streets would be dark and empty. All the Sicilians stayed in their houses with their families. People would stay out, going to bars and restaurants mainly in the summer months, so the only place the porter could have a social life was at work. Going to work, and staying in the reception area, he was likely to meet interesting people, whereas at home, he would be sitting on a couch, watching TV, and going to bed at 9 p.m.

The porter preferred to keep in touch with the rest of the world through meeting clients of different nationalities. He didn't want to be limited only to his Mediterranean island, he wanted make contact with the whole globe. His life was so divided in two, firstly a life at night in the hotel, and secondly a life at home during the day.

His desire to stay at the hotel at night was also due to his poor contacts and rare meetings with the opposite sex. The social life in the village in the summer was limited to an unexciting walk in the village square, the villagers would parade up and down all evening. He found *la passeggiata* (the promenade) rather old-fashioned, compared to the Nordic methods of meeting people in crowded pubs, so he never went for the Sunday walk in the square.

A family friend once gave Luca a telephone number and told him to phone a girl. He did, chatted to her for a while and then asked her out. To his surprise, she accepted, and so later he collected her in his old white car, and took her to a different village. She was very thin with blue eyes and long brown curly shoulder-length hair. She was well dressed. He took her to a bar and bought her ice cream. They sat talking for a while, and he later took her home. He repeated the same thing the next weekend: took her out with the car to the next village, to another bar, bought her an ice cream then took her to her own home. The porter got to know her well after a while, but the outings were always the same. There was a drive in the car for miles and miles, to a bar, ice cream then home again. When the porter asked if she wanted to get out of the car to go for a walk, she always refused. She refused to get out of the car in her own village and confessed that she did not want to be seen in public with a strange man. Her reputation of being a 'good' girl would be ruined.

Luca felt very restricted; his outings in the car became monotonous. He felt he wasn't making any progress with her – not enough to start a physical relationship, anyhow. The next time they sat at a table to eat an ice cream, the porter made a comment on her skinny hands. He didn't mean to be hurtful, but he did end up hurting her feelings. He told her she was too skinny all over, and that she should drink more milk, fatten up a bit. He meant it to be a suggestion, a piece of constructive advice, but the girl took offence. He actually thought that she looked anorexic; if only she would fatten up a bit she would look much better. But alas, Luca had not learnt from past experience – that it's not always good to say what you think.

Luca was later introduced to another woman, a gymnast, who was very thin too. She had short brown hair and dark brown eyes, with an attractive complexion. She generally dressed in a tracksuit. On their first date, they went walking along the beach. It was July, the stars were out, the moon was big and reflecting its light over the surface of the sea, and it all seemed very romantic. The boats and the fishermen were out at sea and there was a warm breeze in the air. The gymnast was a dreamy type. She wrote a poem for Luca and named it after a bird of some sort. She was one of those people that were in love with the idea of being in love. The porter didn't like thin women, and the ones he met all seemed to want to emulate those supermodels that you see on TV. But this girl was not a supermodel but a down-to-earth gym teacher. She invited the porter to the gym whilst her students were still there all exercising under her directions, and when they all left, the gymnast and porter spent some moments together. The girl even got Luca to do some exercises, to loosen his muscles. But after the leg and arm stretching, they both sat down amongst the gym equipment and had a talk and few moments of relaxation and physical closeness. The meetings at the gymnasium went on for several weeks. She told him she had two brothers. She said that they were very protective of her, wouldn't let anyone near her, and that they possessed the short *lupara* type of shotgun, which they often used for hunting wild animals in the local area, and she hinted that they wouldn't hesitate to use the gun on anyone who hurt her.

The porter and gymnast went out for long car rides, and rarely walked in the open together or anywhere where she could be seen by friends or neighbours. On one occasion he drove her home, parked the car in the central car park, switched off the engine, and they just sat there for a while. They talked as usual, and just before Luca was about to kiss her on the cheek to say goodnight, a local coach full of passengers drove by right in front of the parked car. The gymnast suddenly jerked away from Luca, not wanting him to reach out and kiss her. He remained astonished, surprised at her immediate withdrawal. He asked her what the matter was. Surely, he thought, he did not have bad breath, smell of garlic or have terrible body odour. He definitely was not dirty and malodorous; he had a shower every single day. What was the matter? He thought about it and asked her. She had moved away from his approaching face because, she said, she did not want her village friends or neighbours to see her being kissed on the cheek by a stranger.

That would be a scandal, and she would never hear the end of it and would be stigmatised as the village prostitute. She was so terrified that it left Luca bewildered. He suddenly got the impression that he was living in an Arab country, where women's faces are hidden away behind veils.

Paris

One day, the gymnast had been an hour late for the appointment at the gym. Luca was exceptionally tired, as he had had a long and stressful night at work. They entered the gymnasium and spent about half an hour together, when suddenly she said she had to go, she had to go and meet her mother at the market. The porter at that point unexpectedly lost his temper. She had never seen him in a bad temper, and so she became perturbed. He said in an angry tone, 'On no account call me here just for half an hour – I must get some sleep!' That sudden outburst of temper seemed to put an end to the sweet and short relationship, because after he said that in a severe tone, she remained disillusioned.

The train continued on its steady march towards Paris. Luca still sat there gazing out of the window. Occasionally he opened his sports bag, and took a small plastic bottle of water out to have a quick drink. He really didn't quite know where he was; it was sufficient for him to know that he was going to Paris. The Indian man, who had been sitting beside him, had gone to sit with some friends further down the carriage. The porter was sitting alone now. He resumed his thoughts and gave himself a half smile when he thought back to another woman, his dentist.

The porter hated going to the dentist, but had to go at some stage. The dentist was a very clever woman, tall and strong looking. She was not eye-catching but she had a strong personality. He liked her for that reason, but he had heard that she was quite depressed, and as a good turn, he had offered to take her out, to

Paris

dine out, to eat a pizza somewhere. The message got through to the dentist, but nothing came of it. She never got in touch with him.

Days later, a knock on the door had woken the porter as he was taking his morning sleep. He opened the front door, and saw two women standing there. They introduced themselves, and said they were the dentist's friends. They had come to meet the porter, and suggested he should go along with them and the dentist for a small holiday in a hotel somewhere. This was pretty strange, but Luca quickly accepted.

After a few days, the porter received a phone call from the dentist. She phoned to see if he'd accepted the invitation, and to see what arrangements had to be made. 'Good, then, we shall all go for a week to Taormina, share a room and hope to have a good time!'

The porter was astounded at the quick decision and speedy organisation. He was also suddenly exited at the idea of sharing a room with two or three other women – something he had never done before.

One of the women had dropped out, but the dentist and her short friend were all too willing to go ahead with the mini-break at the local holiday town of Taormina.

The day soon arrived; the dentist came and parked outside the porter's house. She had a nice green Alfa Romeo. She came to the door, rang the bell and made sure that the porter was ready to go with them.

At the hotel they brought their luggage in and settled in, and checked that the room and beds were all right. There was a double and a single bed in the room, but no air conditioning.

Paris

Luca, in a way, wanted to pursue the dentist, to chat her up and to flirt with her, but she did not seem a bit interested. Instead, it was her friend, the girl with short brown hair, dark brown eyes and dark skin, who did all the chatting and chasing after Luca! She followed him, kept very close to him, and always had something to say to him.

They went to the beach during the day, and during the evening went out to a restaurant or pizzeria. All three of them walked around everywhere together.

They also went to see a show in a gay nightclub club, to watch transvestites sing and dance on the stage and perform. It was all very amusing and entertaining.

Back at the hotel, nothing exciting happened; they all just went to bed to sleep. The two women slept in the double bed, and the porter in the single bed, and throughout the night, Luca could only contemplate how he might introduce himself cheekily into the women's' double bed without getting rejected or kicked out.

Only after the holiday had finished, and all three went back to their respective homes, did the dentist's friend get in touch with the porter.

She went on another holiday and sent Luca a postcard. She started to phone him incessantly, and in the end, Luca succumbed and asked her out. He asked her to go for a pizza or a drink with him. He collected her, and they went for picturesque drives along the coast to look at and admire the scenery. They sometimes parked the car and spent some time together.

In December, the nights were shorter and darker. The short woman started to make excuses that she had to be at home early, that her father did not like her to stay out late any more, and, just like Cinderella, she was ordered to be in the house by midnight.

Again, Luca was tired, his one and only night off did not allow him to unwind from the stress accumulated over the previous nights. So his tiredness made him lose his temper; he thought that the woman was simply making excuses for not staying out late any more. But, very probably, it was not an excuse. Some women in Italy live at home, even after thirty years of age, and do as their parents ask. However the porter lost his patience, and temper yet again. And when that happened, it surely frightened away the prey for ever. Though she continued to repeat that her father wanted her back in the house by midnight, the porter continued to disbelieve her. He thought she was trying to end the relationship for some other reason. So, in anticipation, the mentally and physically exhausted porter told her in no ambiguous terms that he didn't love her. 'I don't love you – do you understand?'

At least this time the porter would end the relationship, not the other way round, where it's the female to do it first. Luca realised later, however, that he had made a mistake, reacting like that. His excessive tiredness, caused by never catching up on his sleep, made him suddenly change his personality. He became impatient, even aggressive at times, very sensitive and easily upset.

That was, and sometimes still is, the situation in small Sicilian villages. Women have to keep a close eye on their movements in public. They must not be seen in public with men, or else there will be subject to village gossip. The friends and neighbours would brand them as the village good-for-nothing tarts.

In the hotel where he worked, the old woman, Donna Francesca, who kept on banging on the hotel doors at five in the morning, had a young family friend. The girl was in her thirties, and still was without a stable fiancé or boyfriend; at least that is what everyone believed, or was told to believe. The old woman frequently talked about her young friend, telling the porter how fine she was, in the sense that she was still a chaste, untouched woman. The elderly woman often remarked to Luca that there were no more virgin women in the city; that her friend was the last decent, fresh virgin still in circulation.

She seemed quite convinced about it. She spoke disapprovingly of other women, saying that they were indecent; that they would be seen on the streets at night with boys on their motorbikes. It was obvious that the old woman was trying hard to recommend her friend to the porter. She didn't say it straight out, but she would have been pleased for her friend to be coupled with the concierge.

The friend worked in the hotel too. She arrived in the morning at 7 a.m. on the dot, but as she arrived the porter would go home, and so they never really had a chance to meet. On the very rare occasions when they did meet and talk, Donna Francesca's friend proved to be an extremely shy woman. She was probably brought up to believe that all men are bad, and that she must keep away from them. The porter had heard from other sources that the girl's father had stopped her from seeing a man she obviously liked or loved. He

Paris

put an end to their relationship, forbade his daughter from ever seeing this man again, probably on the grounds that the young woman's fiancé was not a prince.

Luca tried at times to talk to her, but never got a response. She seemed to have no initiative or will to start any new relationship. She just smiled, went about her daily work and never made an effort to make friends. Luca thought that she had probably been educated to believe that men like shy, quiet women, that men saw quiet women as a sign of a 'good' wife. The porter was never quite sure whether the woman was shy on purpose, trying to be attractive to the opposite sex, and get them interested, or simply because she was really shy and afraid; afraid to start a new relationship because she hadn't got over the last one that her father forcefully terminated.

One evening, the porter managed to get her to keep him company in the reception hall. They sat together behind the desk and had a friendly talk. She was a simple, pretty woman with short fair hair and dark brown eyes, almost looking like a nurse in her hotel uniform. She had very little to say; she had a nice smile but always seemed a little uncomfortable. She didn't want hotel clients to see that she was there talking to the porter.

Luca often asked her to go out, to go for a pizza somewhere, but the woman kept on saying, 'We will one day, we will go out, but not now.' Her response was always the same, she kept on delaying, till after many years, he gave up and stopped asking. Luca found her to be very quiet and calm and mysterious.

Paris

He wondered if all this 'goody-goody' façade was hiding a different kind of person. Was she in reality a sex-starved woman? Or was she already getting her fair share of sexual adventures from some unknown individual? Was the person well known and working in the hotel? Was the man keeping her sexually satisfied? Was the man a married man? The porter often felt she was having sex during working hours. As she was a chambermaid and her job was to clean all the hotel rooms, and also to work in the hot and noisy hotel laundry, couldn't it be possible, he thought, that one of the male personnel could be having sex with her, in the laundry or in one of the bedrooms?

The mysterious man could be a respectable married man, and there he was, in the hotel in his honest job, doing a favour to the hard-up virgin of the city. He had his wife at home, his mistress at work, and she had her needs fulfilled as well as maintaining a virginal façade. The porter had a strong suspicion that something was going on. He had never met such a cold and detached woman. Or was the woman only interested in other women? She wouldn't go out with him because she was too busy with her female friends! Of course, he did also consider that she was not interested in him, or, more likely, that she was still secretly seeing her outlawed fiancé.

The train continued speeding towards Paris, but Luca was oblivious to what was going on around him. There were some passengers talking away on the other seats. He did not take any notice of then. He did not even notice what he was looking at outside. His eyes were looking out, but he did not see anything. He was too deep in thought.

The porter thought back to another woman he'd been introduced to. A family neighbour and friend had invited the porter one day to go with her to meet a young girl. The porter, having nothing to do that day, had decided to go with the old woman, their neighbour, mainly out of curiosity to see what kind of blind date she was fixing up for him.

The old neighbour was a sturdy type; she spent her life working in a big hotel, but also spent a lot of her spare time working in the fields, cultivating her modest vegetable plot. She was unrefined and strong, as most widows turn out to be after living alone for many years. She invited the porter with enthusiasm and persuaded him to meet this girl; she wanted to do well and be responsible for fixing up another young couple.

They went to the town together and walked to a place where the girl was working – in a small house behind a ceramics shop situated on the main street. The porter waited outside in the lane whilst the old woman went to the house to find the young woman. She disappeared into a house for quite some time, and the porter thought that the old woman could not convince the young woman to come out and meet the porter. But the two women finally emerged. The porter was expecting, well... he didn't know what to expect, but when he saw the female emerge from the door of the house, he was taken aback.

She was tall, not bad looking, but it was her general appearance that astounded him. She appeared to be dressed like an old woman, as if she had spent most of her life with the mature folk of the town. She had a long shawl over her shoulders to keep her warm, wore an old, long dark skirt and long socks, and her shoes were a horrible coffee colour. Her hair had no style; there was nothing modern about her. She reluctantly came out of the house, as if only to obey the old woman. She was visibly very shy and reserved, nervous too. Looking even closer, Luca noticed she had quite a round enlarged stomach. He immediately thought that the old woman was getting him to meet an expectant woman. But there was no escaping now. He came to meet her; they were both now there in the street, with the old woman acting as the mediator.

After the first introductory meeting, Luca felt that the young woman seemed to be in a profound gloom. It was as if she had reached the stage where life had lost all its interest and meaning for her. Her eyes were lifeless and dull, and only occasionally did she give a required smile.

After some thought he decided he would take her out, if only to try to give a new lease of life. They exchanged telephone numbers and he agreed that he would get in touch with her. Deep down, she seemed pleased about the newly acquired friend, but kept her pleasure hidden and low-key.

After a few days the porter phoned and agreed to meet her in the town square. They met early in the evening in the central piazza. There were many people walking around, hoards of tourists in their modern outfits, but there she was, in her old-fashioned clothes, as if she'd stepped straight out of a museum wearing the museum's historic garments.

They walked the crowded street together, talking. From one end of the lane they went to the other, turned around and repeated the walk. She worked nights too, she told the porter. She looked after an old woman; she slept in a bed next to the old woman and kept an eye on her from about 9 p.m. till the next morning. She was employed as a kind of personal nurse. Thereafter, Luca and the woman met regularly and did the same walk every time. They walked the same steps, went down the same alleyways, and sat on the same benches when they got tired. Again, like the other Sicilian women, she avoided walking past certain places so as not to be seen by someone she knew. It was not 'like her' to be walking in the street with a man next to her, she remarked. A friend or a relative would gossip, or make fun of her the next time they met. So again, as with the other women, Luca had the distinct feeling he and she were another pair of fugitives, like two newly escaped prisoners who had to keep out of the spotlight. It was ridiculous! Every time Luca met a woman, they all had the same fear – the fear of being seen and talked about.

They met and walked together; at other times they talked on the phone for long hours. Luca in due course discovered that her diet consisted mainly of pasta, every single day; no wonder she had a big round stomach, looking like a pregnant woman. In time, she must have eventually changed her diet, because she gradually became thinner.

Bit by bit, she changed her clothing from the old-fashioned, old woman's outfit to a more modern-day style. She started to dress more sexily, and wore more black.

She told Luca that she had very strict religious parents, that she had led a secluded life at home and that she had never gone on holidays or on outings. Luca pressed her to become more mobile, become more independent, to buy and drive a car. When they got to know each other better, she opened up and told him of her past experiences with married men, men who would come up to her whilst she was waiting at the bus stop, and propose themselves to her. The men would cheekily suggest a relationship, sexual or otherwise, but she told Luca that she always refused a married man's advances. She added that she didn't like any of the men that came up to her anyway. When the conversation got more personal, she confessed that she was a virgin. Well, well, Luca thought, everyone in Sicily is a virgin!

Eventually Luca got bored with just walking up and down the street, over and over again. When he proposed to her to go and sit in a bar to drink a coffee, or to go to eat something in the restaurant, the woman always refused. At a table they could talk over a nice meal; but no, she utterly refused, she could eat at home if she was hungry, she said. Again, like all the other Sicilian women, she was frightened of being seen by friends or relatives.

It was clear that Luca was not lucky with the indigenous islanders. Perhaps he did not have the right technique; perhaps he was too much of a gentleman. He was not aggressive, or bold, or cheeky. He was not like a close relative of his, who, every time he opened his mouth, came out with the right phrases; this man was able to flirt with and seduce any woman. The porter often wondered where he learnt his methods from, from which school. Either the porter did not have the right method, was not bold enough, or simply he was unfortunate in always meeting peculiar women who were afraid of letting themselves go.

Luca not only had this setback with the women in Sicily, but also with the woman he had known in his three years in Milan.

There he had met quite an attractive woman, a teacher who was quite an eye-catcher. Luca heard that she had many men after her, many proposals, but all of them fell through. She was not happy with any of the men she met. There was something about this woman teacher that really got the males to stand at attention, to look at her when she walked by. She could have been a model if she had been thinner; she had the face and body, she dressed well and she really was quite impressive. When Luca first met her, he was almost hypnotised by her femininity, by her sexuality. She had long dark brown hair, big brown eyes; she moved and talked with grace, and was gentle in her ways. Her gentle, soft tone of voice helped to melt the men she talked to. She was a 'sex bomb'; she could have had any man she wanted.

Luca was impressed; most men were impressed with her attractive appearance. He made friends with her, and gradually got to know her better, but it was a very difficult and slow process.

In the initial stages, Luca tried to go out with her, beginning with the difficult and repeated phone calls he made to her. She was never in, or she was in the bathroom and he was told to call back later. Teachers are generally regarded as respectable women; they are not supposed to give in easily and quickly to a man's advances. The more Luca kept on trying to get her to go out with him, the more the sexy tutor always came up with excuses. One alleged reason, which came up often, was the one where she said she had an aching stomach, or a headache. She often had a bad tummy, and Luca often asked himself, what on earth was she eating?

After several months the woman eventually agreed to go out with Luca, but there was always a 'but'. She would not be alone; she said, she would bring friends of hers along too. She suggested that they go on an outing and have a good time somewhere.

One weekend, the sex symbol teacher brought two other friends along with her. The other couple had a sports car, and so all four went to Lake Como for the day in that car. Her friends were bizarre. The young, hippy-looking man was a bad and dangerous driver. He had long hair and dark glasses. His short girlfriend was a strange type too, always stuttering when she spoke, and could barely see out of her John Lennon specs.

The outings became regular, but the teacher later brought different friends along with her. Luca and the teacher never managed to go out unaccompanied together, as he wanted to. On one occasion, she brought a group of handicapped friends with her. Luca had nothing against handicapped people, but when was she going to let him go out with her alone? It seemed never. This was happening in Milan, not in some small Sicilian village. There seemed to be no difference between the mentalities of the two localities, the south of Italy and the more prosperous north. Either there is this all-round position regarding Italian women, or somebody had put a curse on Luca, rendering him slippery and unfortunate and repellent and negative in the eyes of Mediterranean females.

As time progressed, they eventually started to go out together alone. But, too much time had gone by, probably a year and a half. They were now getting to know each other quite well, but it was a long, slow process. It was like watching a slow motion movie. In a way, they were similar, slow and afraid to make risky moves. They had a similar attitude to life, and lived at a similar unhurried pace.

They eventually went on very long bike trips out of the city, or for very long walks from the outskirts of town to the centre. Luca's shoes wore out in no time, and his backside became sore after riding the bike for miles. It definitely was not an easy courtship – if you could call it that. It was time-consuming and demanding. Luca's patience often reached its limit.

They started to use an old car to go out. But most of the time she, the host, native to the city, did not know where to go. They would set out and just drive for miles, back and forth, turning left then right, going down streets that ended up nowhere. In reality, she didn't know her own town, didn't know where to go. They eventually went to a club to listen to jazz music. On another night they went to see a theatrical musical, a topless play. And on another occasion they went to a communist rally, held outdoors, where it poured down with rain, and they got soaked to the bone.

Paris

Time flew by, first days, then months. It just seemed that this woman was determined to be difficult, to play hard to get, to play her role as a respectful, clean, family woman; but by the end of the third year, it all had to end. Luca had had enough of Milan and all that was in it. He threw in the towel, gave up and transferred to Sicily.

After several years, when the relationship seemed dead and buried, the teacher decided to go down to Sicily to meet Luca, to have a holiday near the beach; but even then she did not come alone. She had to bring a friend with her who seemed to have lesbian tendencies. Somebody up there, in the heavens, had already decided that a relationship between Luca and the schoolteacher was not to be! Every attempt at the two to be together seemed to fail unhappily.

Luca introduced the teacher's friend to a Sicilian friend of his, hoping that he would take her out, take her to a different beach or restaurant, so that Luca and the teacher could be alone together. It was soon apparent that it would be difficult to keep the two women separated, they were always looking for each other and always seem to want to be together. Had the teacher changed, Luca thought? Was she secretly always like that, even in Milan? Luca was surprised, now, to think that she may have had these lesbian tendencies all the time, but he came to the conclusion that perhaps they were just really close friends. Finally, one day the porter lured the teacher away, early in the morning, to a quiet rocky beach, hoping to get her away from the other couple before they woke up and got up. Little did the porter know that the stretch of beach that he chose, full of big boulders and rocks, was the beach favoured by homosexuals...

In fact, behind every big rock or boulder, there was a couple of males, lying there taking in the sun, lying on their towels and spreading sun cream on each other.

The porter and the teacher spent the day on that beach, disregarding the homosexuals around them. It was the closest that Luca had ever been to the schoolteacher. They spent the day swimming in the sea in a secluded spot between the rocks, sunbathing, talking of past experiences, and generally getting physically and spiritually closer. Out of the blue, he sensitively and uncontrollably kissed her smooth, sensual, sea-scented neck, instantly melting the ice within her and making his sun-drenched Sicilian blood boil.

By evening, when the sun was going down behind the mountains, Luca decided to go for a car ride with her. They gathered their beach gear, got in the car, and he drove her up a meandering road and went to a quiet path just outside a beautiful hilltop village called Forza D'Agró near Taormina. He parked the car in a secluded area, near a cemetery in fact, and nobody was around, it seemed at first. Luca was finally alone with the teacher. Looking around outside the car, all you could see was the far away beach and mountains. The stretch of road seemed desolate.

The couple tried to be comfortable in the car. They sat in the front seat, adjusted the seats so they were in the lying down position, looked at each other, and then, just as his hands were caressing and exploring her tanned, silky, sensual body, just as the pair were getting physically impassioned, an old man and young boy and his dog appeared round the corner and started to walk in the direction of the couple's car. The porter calmly stopped what he was about to do; he composed himself, switched the car engine on and slowly drove away from the scene. The couple never had another opportunity to be alone again. A few days later the teacher and her friend went back to Milan.

Luca wondered what had happened to the sensual schoolteacher. Where did she end up? He had heard a rumour that she got married, but the news was not definite. He thought how strange it was, how life was strange, meeting new people all the time, for a brief moment, for a day, a week, a month or year, only to see them disappear... disappear into the past, and out of your life.

Luca looked at his mobile phone. There was a message from Katherine, saying that she was no longer in Ireland, but that she was already sitting comfortably in a hotel room in Paris. It had taken her just over an hour to fly from Dublin to Paris. She had expected the porter to be in Paris already, to arrive there before she did, but missing the train at Rome had caused his late arrival. She knew that he had missed the connection at Rome, but she was patient, and willing to wait.

The porter sat back and made himself more comfortable. At every French station the porter stood up and looked outside the window, and stretched his legs by walking up and down the corridor. It was dark and the weather seemed to be getting worse. It seemed to rain more the further north the train went. It was not

Paris

far to Paris. He sent a text message to his woman friend in Paris to say where he was and to tell her the approximate time of arrival at Bercy Station in the French capital. He advised her to sit and wait in the hotel room, as he would make his own way from the station to the hotel.

The porter sat down and returned to his thoughts. He still had time to go back to his past, to his time spent in the hot sunny island of Sicily. The ticket inspector passed again and mentioned that the weather ahead was expected to get very wet and windy, and that there might be a delay, depending on the situation.

The porter sat back and transported himself back in time; he had a few more hours before arriving at Paris, a small time left for reflection.

Although his job in Sicily meant he was always stuck behind a reception desk, it did not mean he did not travel the world. His job enabled him to meet people from all over the globe, and he remembered in particular some of the women he had met, the ones who stopped at the reception desk to converse with him.

He remembered the friendly Scottish woman who admitted that she loved watching men playing football. She loved the sport, and knew everything about the game and about her home team, Hibernian FC. She was a great football supporter and said that she often went to watch her home team play at the stadium. She said she was used to mixing in with Scottish soccer supporters. She was a fanatical tomboy type, Luca remembered. She was willing to spend the whole night down in the reception hall, talking with the porter, sitting on the hard old rocking chair, chatting and trying to flirt with Luca. She had no worries, no qualms about being seen by the other hotel clients going in and out, or even about being seen by her own close friends. Rather than take a walk in the village street, she would sit in the armchair situated in the foyer in front of the reception desk. She eventually invited Luca to go out for a meal with her on his night off.

Months later, there was a young Austrian who was also very forward and outgoing. She was quite pretty, and one evening on returning from her walk in the Sicilian tourist-clad town, she brought back two small bottles of wine. She asked the porter to open the bottles so she could drink the wine there, in the hall together with the porter. They were only small bottles, so there was no chance of either of them getting drunk. She was lonely, so she kept the porter company, night after night, for two weeks, talking and flirting with him behind the reception desk.

One night, when all the hotel clients, including the Austrian woman, were apparently in their beds, and all seemed quiet, with the hotel lights switched off and doors shut, the porter heard the patter of bare feet coming down the flight of sixty steps. Hurrying round the staircase down to the semi-dark foyer was the Austrian in her nightgown. She was almost nude. She very much reminded the porter of the erotic ghost that appeared in his dreams, only this time she was real, in the flesh. She was not at all embarrassed to be moving about in the hotel corridors and up and down the steps in her flimsy, transparent nightgown. The highly-

Paris

spirited, lonely Austrian sat on the porter's lap, flirted with and encouraged him, temped and seduced him, giving him permission, and the go-ahead to maul and molest her.

The porter also recalled another woman, a tall German girl. She did not speak a word of English, and he did not speak a word of German. Communication between the two was almost entirely in sign language. She always had a big smile on her face, always said '*Ja*' to everything, and always gave the porter the sense that she understood every word he said, when in reality she understood nothing. She was taller than him, blonde and quite attractive. She looked a little like a famous top model and could very well have been a model herself. She would go to the beach and lie there all day without saying a word; she looked emotionally fragile and very shy.

Luca had wanted to be more physical, but was wondering if such a move would destroy their fragile new relationship. So he'd kept his distance and behaved in a gentlemanly way, i.e. cool and detached. Was she expecting a hot Italian to take her, there on the beach? Take her in her arms and make love to her? Luca was always cautious, never really took any outrageous risks, so there the two were, lying on the beach for hours, saying very little to each other. Her face was expressionless and motionless, facing the sky, taking in the heat of the sun, and as he lay on a beach towel beside her, he would stare at her body, her facial features, wishing he could have the guts to break the ice and make the first move, to make headway and touch her. Would she sit up and whack him across the face and tell him to get lost – in her own language, of course? He decided not to try, not yet anyway. He didn't want to make a fool of himself on the beach in front of other local people who knew him and who were there too, on the beach, soaking up the sun.

However, they did get to say a few words to each other, although with great difficulty.

Luca discovered that her diet consisted of fruit and nothing else. Day after day she would only eat fruit, and that's what kept her so thin and healthy.

He also found out that she was a bit of an adventuress. She told him in both broken English and German words, and with signs, that in the past she had jumped from an aeroplane; she had done parachute jumping.

What courage she must have had to jump out of an aeroplane, to let herself go, to let herself fall to earth with a mere parachute strapped to her back, to her thin, tall body. Luca could imagine her diving through the air at incredible speed, plummeting down to the ground, cutting through the cold invisible ocean of air, with her face distorting under the force of the wind. The porter thought, What if? What if the parachute didn't work? What if it didn't open? What a risk to take! What courage! If it didn't open, if the folded parachute didn't unfasten from that backpack, the brave adventurous airborne human bird would turn into a helpless, terrified, plummeting human penguin.

Luca met all sorts. This German girl was another strange being. One evening when they were sitting in the small back garden, adjacent to the railway line, attempting to have a talk in either broken English or German, the woman got a fright. She saw a kitten appear from behind a bush. The kitten was thin and dishevelled. Kittens often came and went. The porter would try to feed and look after them, bring them back to life from certain starvation and death, but it just so happened that at that very moment, a starving kitten in poor physical appearance and condition came out from nowhere and started to wail and meow aloud.

Luca was speechless but so was the German. She must have immediately thought that the cat belonged to Luca, that he was cruel to animals and that he would be cruel to women too. What would she have thought if she was in the garden the day Luca saw a trail of blood leading to the open shed, leading to the back of the spent old washing machine and leading to the whimpering sound of a stray white cat that was curled up in the dark corner, trembling in shock, in evident agony and bleeding to death? The flesh of one of the cat's hind legs had been completely ripped off, revealing a protruding thighbone. Perhaps the cat's leg had been shredded off by a wild dog after a savage fight, or the cat had got its leg accidentally trapped at the nearby railway junction, between the moveable converging railway tracks and had had its leg severed by a passing train.

The German got up abruptly, nearly falling off the chair, and demanded they leave. What strange sudden behaviour, the porter thought; she was not even willing to wait to see if he had an explanation. She must have thought that Luca was a covert maniac, or a sadistic murderer. In reality, the porter loved animals, cats and dogs. The German, because of her lack of communication, and relying too much on her vision, believed and told herself that she was in the wrong

Paris

company. It really was strange behaviour, especially after the woman had spent the last couple of years sending the porter beautiful letters and pictorial cards from Nürnberg. Women's minds must work in strange ways, he thought. The next day, the porter took her to the airport, never to see her again.

WHERE ARE YOU NOW? said the message on the porter's mobile phone.

I AM STILL ON THE TRAIN, he replied with another text message. WHAT ARE YOU DOING IN THE HOTEL?

I AM GOING TO HAVE A SHOWER, was the reply from Paris.

The porter's thoughts of his past escapades were now mingling with the thoughts of meeting his old friend, Katherine, from Ireland. Like a recorded film or tape, the reel was nearing the conclusion. A thought, then a message on his mobile, another thought, another message. The messages were coming through.

The porter looked out of the window and could not see a thing. It was pitch black outside. Occasionally a street lamp could be seen, but it was clear that the train was still a few miles from Paris.

WHAT TIME WILL YOU ARRIVE?

I DON'T KNOW, POSSIBLY AT 1 A.M. I WILL MAKE MY OWN WAY TO THE HOTEL…

OK, SEE YOU IN A WHILE. NOT FAR TO GO. LOVE YOU!

What a great craze this mobile phone is, thought Luca. Modern technology had made great leaps. With a few text messages, he could economically keep in

Paris

touch with someone thousands of miles away, to think that this reunion with his old friend was made possible because of the quick, instant, inexpensive messaging system of the mobile telephone. He could get in touch with someone, miles away, even in another country by simply texting a message.

It had started with an experiment, conducted some time previously. Luca had wanted to see if he could get in touch with Katherine by writing a text with his new mobile phone. At first it was like writing a message in a bottle, and throwing it at sea, hoping to get a reply from someone, somewhere. The porter had typed his message: HELLO, IS ANYBODY THERE? ARE YOU GETTING THIS MESSAGE?

He'd held his new mobile phone in the palm of his hand and marvelled at such a small object that could communicate with someone else. It was wireless too. It had a small screen to accommodate the text messages. He had never used one before, but everyone was buying a mobile phone, so he'd thought, why not get one himself.

He looked patiently at the screen, not really expecting to see anything. How could such a small object send and receive a text message in a few seconds to another part of the world? He knew how, he knew about satellites, but he still thought it was magic. The old telephone with the wire was magic too, but you could not send text messages. This wireless gadget was something new. There was still no answer on his mobile screen. Either she was still ignoring him or he had typed in the wrong telephone number. She had been ignoring him for a long time, had stopped answering his letters. She had become fed up with letter writing; perhaps the phone would get her to reply. He tried typing in her telephone number again, typing in the correct international code number first. He waited and waited. He also thought that perhaps she had changed her mobile and so had changed her telephone number too. In that case there was no hope. He would have lost contact with her completely. It felt like the execution of an old friend, the death of somebody you knew well.

A few minutes elapsed, and just as he was putting his new cellphone in his pocket, the frog croaked, his mobile croaked. There it was, written in big black capital letters:

ONE MESSAGE RECEIVED

He opened the message, and it was, to his great surprise, a reply from Ireland. His message was received and now he was getting the answer. The message system worked even for great distances. He was surprised but also exhilarated at getting a message back from someone he once knew so well. It then felt as if his friend had come back to life – a strange feeling.

YES, I AM GETTING YOUR MESSAGE.

Messages started to ping-pong back and forth. It felt good to be able to communicate with someone and get an immediate reaction, an instant reply, rather than wait for days for a letter, and both Luca and Katherine were weary of letter writing.

WHERE ARE YOU AND WHAT ARE YOU DOING? Luca wrote.

Paris

I AM IN THE BOG COLLECTING TURF!

COLLECTING TURF? WHAT'S TURF? WHERE? IN THE BOG? WHAT'S THE BOG?

TURF! IT'S A FUEL SIMILAR TO COAL, YOU BURN IT IN THE FIRE FOR THE WINTER. THE BOG IS THE BLACK FIELDS WHERE YOU COLLECT THE TURF! WHERE ARE YOU AND WHAT ARE YOU UP TO?

I AM IN THE GARDEN TRYING THIS NEW PHONE OUT. BEEN OUT ON THE BEACH ALL DAY. VERY HOT HERE.

Luca was no longer in Sicily, but was approaching Paris. Soon he and Katherine would stop texting, and soon would be face-to-face and talking directly to each other. But he had to admit that the little new mobile phones helped make the long journey from Sicily a little easier.

Using the text message helped two people living far away from each other to keep in touch relatively cheaply. Luca thought it was a great simple way of keeping in touch.

He thought momentarily of another Irishwoman he'd met a few years ago, again in the hotel where he was employed. In contrast, she had not liked sending text messages; she claimed that the new method of communicating was mainly used by the younger generation, not by adults.

The tall, slightly hefty blonde woman had walked into the hotel with two other tall, dark and thin Irishwomen. She'd seen Luca and immediately there had been eye contact. The fact that the porter spoke good English helped to ease the newly arrived holidaymakers' nervousness. They were afraid that they would have difficulties in a foreign country because they were not able to speak the language. Finding an English-speaking porter on arrival helped them to settle down. The three Irishwomen promptly made friends with him. They asked him for information on the local town and events in the area, on the excursions available to them. Sooner or later they ended up talking for a long time on other subjects as the porter stood behind his hotel reception desk, and the three girls standing on the other side of it.

The first time they came to Sicily they only stayed for two weeks. The three girls were always together during the day on the beach, and at night they would go out to eat in one of the many Sicilian restaurants in the hilltop town. It was on their last night in the hotel that the blonde came down to the reception hall by herself and tried to be extra friendly with Luca. Like other interested women seemed to do, she came down to the lobby, and asked Luca if she could buy a bottle of water. On receiving the bottle in her hand, she then asked him to open the bottle for her. It seemed to Luca that the bottle-opening sequence was a kind of international body language. If they were interested in any way in the porter, the women would ask for a bottle, or bring their own bottle and ask him to open it for them. Luca, with time and experience, noticed and deduced that this bottle-opening run was the women's way of saying, 'Hey, I fancy you... I want *you*.'

Luca's way of holding the bottle in his hand, the way in which he took off the bottle top for his clients, right in front of them, seemed to suggest he was

Paris

getting the message sent to him by the woman standing in front of him. She was giving him a wake-up call, she was sending the message, and he was receiving it and replying with the appropriate bottle language. The message, without the use of words or signs, was in the bottle-opening act. It seemed like a kind of commonly understood signal used by women. If they asked the porter to open a bottle for them, it was their hint to him that they wanted something other than a bottle of water. The porter did not always rely solely on the bottle signal; he surely would be in trouble if he did. There were other gestures involved, such as eye or hand contacts.

The blonde looked at him and smiled, took the opened bottle and said her goodbyes. She told him how much she enjoyed staying in the hotel and thanked him for all his help. She turned and went up to her room, and a few minutes later she rang Luca at the reception and in a very friendly manner suggested that they keep in touch and exchange addresses. She said she would send him a postcard from her home country, Ireland.

About a month later, the first postcard arrived from Ireland, then a little later another one arrived, then another. They kept on coming: Christmas cards, birthday cards, Easter cards, beautiful colourful cards… Some were very artistic, pictures of animals, horses in particular. Then the letters started to arrive, on beautifully headed paper. The letters were written with passion and enthusiasm; some of them were very long. Veronica, the German parachute jumper, and Sonia, the Irish blonde, were great card and letter writers.

Then came the phone calls, but Luca replied with text messages. The blonde advised the porter that she was coming back to Sicily for another short holiday, but this time she would be alone, with no friends. She asked Luca if he would be able to show her the sights and keep her company during her brief stay in the holiday town. The porter naturally agreed to be her chaperone for the two weeks.

The blonde booked into a hotel, but not the same one as Luca was working in. She soon phoned Luca at his home to say she had arrived, and so arranged to meet him in her hotel's foyer.

Luca, without delay, arrived and waited in the hotel hallway. A charming little hotel, he thought, bigger and more modern than the one he was working in. He waited about ten minutes, looked at all the pictures on the wall, and observed the hotel staff as clients walked in and out of the hotel.

He had forgotten what the blonde looked like. Two years had passed by since he'd last met her. He had a general idea of her appearance, but could not be precise. The hotel lift doors opened and out came a sturdy-looking blonde woman. She looked around and quickly recognised the porter, walked up to him and they greeted each other and exchanged kisses on the cheeks. She invited him back to her room.

This hotel seemed to be tolerant towards strangers who did not register in the hotel or leave their passports or documents with the receptionist for temporary custody. The blonde and Luca walked straight past the receptionist and into the lift without being stopped for an identification check. Luca was

Paris

surprised at the ease with which he was allowed in the hotel.

They stepped into the lift, the doors closed, and the lift went down. After a few moments, the doors opened and they both stepped out. The blonde then led the way through the corridor, and then out through a door, into a garden, towards what seemed like an outside cabin. It looked like a little hut or chalet. The rest of the hotel was full, so this external chalet in the middle of the hotel garden was all that was available.

The blonde invited him in; they sat down and talked for a while, drinking wine and eating crisps. The chalet was pleasant, there was just enough room for a bed, a TV, a fridge and a table, and there was also a small shower. You could see the wooden panelling and beams on the roof, which made it all look very Scandinavian.

After a few hours of conversation, they both decided to go out for a drink and a meal in one of the many restaurants in the town. She dressed up and put on a very long dress, which nearly touched the floor. Long dresses seemed to suit her, seemed to hide or camouflage her slightly corpulent body. The evening dress really made a difference to her normal daytime appearance. With a bit of red lipstick and eye shadow, the blonde looked like a different person.

She locked the hotel room with her key and went with Luca out of the hotel. They walked into the narrow street and made their way to the central bar. The town was full of tourists, mainly German and Americans, all sitting in bars and restaurants, or simply strolling along the central street looking at all the small ceramics, souvenirs, memorabilia, or at the fashion shops. They sat at a table in a central open-air bar and ordered some drinks. They drank and talked, watched the tourists walk back and forth, and looked at tourists have their faces drawn by the street artists. Later they left the bar and walked to a restaurant to have something to eat. As they talked they got to know each other a little better, and in all they had a pleasant social evening. He later accompanied her back to her hotel room, had another drink with her, and then at about eleven had to leave to go to work.

Luca went back to the hotel chalet the following afternoon, she invited him in again and offered him another drink. They later went out to do some walking around, to stroll around and to visit the Greek theatre. In the evening the Irishwoman seemed quite appealing, all dressed up in her long evening wear, with make-up on her face. She looked quite glamorous, like an actress. Many men looked at her as she walked by; she was a conspicuous figure. During the day however, she lost her magnetism, she dressed normally, in shorts, and a tee shirt and didn't wear any make-up. Her hair didn't seem to have the same shine as the night before.

After looking at the Greek theatre, taking photographs and buying some ceramic souvenirs, they walked back to the hotel chalet. Again, she offered Luca a drink with some crisps. They talked and talked. She switched the TV on, as she knew that the Grand Prix Formula One racing was being transmitted. She loved the sport, she loved racing cars and cars in general and so they lay on the bed watching the race. Circuit after circuit, lap after lap, she lay there on the bed, transfixed by the TV, with the red Ferrari cars which were leading the race. She loved the red Ferraris.

The porter was amazed to see a grown woman being immersed in what is generally regarded as a man's sport. She did, in due course, admit that she loved soccer too. She briefly reminded the porter of the Scottish woman he knew, and the Sicilian gym teacher. They seemed to have something in common – they were keen on male sports.

When the race was over, the blonde woman looked at Luca with a hungry, carnally playful smile, and with Formula One speed, closed the curtains. When she reopened them it was dark outside and the porter had to rush to get to work, which started at midnight. His hotel, his workplace, was within walking distance, but he had to be on duty at midnight.

The following days they continued to see each other. He usually went to the hotel chalet in the afternoon, and stayed there till eleven in the evening. They talked, drank, ate and generally enjoyed each other's company. Towards the end of her stay in Sicily, she invited Luca back to Ireland.

'Come and see me in Ireland,' she said, 'it's a beautiful place, you will love it.'

'Yes, OK,' the porter replied. 'I will one day.'

He already knew that he was unlikely to visit her in Ireland; he already knew he had problems with travelling long distances, and he already had a friend in Ireland – a friend who seemed to live only a few miles

Paris

from her. Still, he didn't want to disappoint her; he simply said he would think about it when the time comes.

The ten days flew by quickly, and the Irishwoman was soon on the plane back to Ireland. After a while, even bigger, more colourful cards started to arrive in the porter's mailbox. Then came longer letters, and then came the phone calls. She would rarely text messages but always phoned. 'Hi, thanks for showing me around and looking after me, I really enjoyed my holiday. I hope you will think about coming over to Ireland.'

'I will, I will,' he replied.

Over time, her phone calls diminished, perhaps because he didn't phone back, perhaps because he only replied by text message.

The train now seemed to be slowing down. The porter looked outside and could now see all the city lights as the train approached Paris. The people on the train were all getting their things ready. Travelling bags were pulled out from luggage shelves above their heads, and most passengers were putting their raincoats on. The train seemed to be slowing down but never stopping. The city was very big and the multitude of street lights made Luca feel a little better, a little less isolated. He had a quick flashback image of the beach in Sicily, of the hot sunny climate there, but it didn't last long. The reality of the cold wet city that was waiting for him outside was staring at him in the face. He too, like all the other travellers, put his jacket on and prepared his luggage.

Paris

Everyone was in commotion. It was a good thing they were not on a plane that was about to land, or else the plane would have rocked from side to side, causing a disaster on the runway. The train was allowing them to get a good view of the French city. The major monuments could be seen in the distance, together with cathedrals and churches. All the prominent buildings were illuminated, including the world famous Eiffel Tower, the top of which seemed to have a searchlight turning round and round, aiming its light in the distance all around.

The train slowed and slowed till it eventually stopped in the station. The train had finally reached its destination. The travellers all queued up in the gangway carrying their bulky luggage. Then, step by step, they made their way towards the train exit.

Luca stepped out on to the platform with his luggage. The cooler air and the humid atmosphere immediately hit him. The mass of people on the platform grabbed their bags and all walked in the direction of the exit. Luca, too, now had to make his way to the hotel where his lady was waiting, the hotel being on the other side of the city. He set off, pulling his luggage behind him till he could find the ticket office. Before queuing up to buy a ticket for the underground, he carefully studied one of the maps of the underground trains that was on the wall for all to see. He studied where he would have to make train changes, and connections.

With the ticket in hand he made his way towards the underground. With a little difficulty, he got past the human toll gates, the ones that only let one person pass through one at a time. Luca put the ticket in the slot that was clearly indicated and illustrated. The machine sucked up the ticket, almost his finger too, and the metal bars that blocked his passage loosened and opened to allow him through. Being with luggage, made the entry procedure a little more complicated, but eventually he worked out how and where he and his luggage were supposed to pass.

Luca had never liked the underground, as he'd had a bad experience with it when he lived in Milan. The Milan underground was quite easy to comprehend, but the Paris underground seemed like a chaotic nightmare. The directional signs were everywhere; they had different names, different colours, different letters or numbers. Unless one knew exactly where one was going, it was easy to make a slip-up and get lost in the underground maze.

After walking for what seemed like miles under the French capital city, Luca finally stepped on to a carriage in an underground train. The carriage was full of people standing or sitting, with their strange faces all looking lifeless and motionless. Some looked bored and really miserable, some stared into the distance; some were not mentally there at all, but were miles away, a few stared at the porter, who was now sweating a little for having walked a great distance pulling his wheeled luggage. It was dark outside the train carriage, but well illuminated inside. The train started and stopped continuously and at times seemed to reach very high speeds, even when it was going round moderate bends.

The train doors opened and closed, and people

Paris

went in and out, all moving like involuntary zombies or robots. They all seemed like a gathering of people without inner souls. One man however, started to speak out loud to everybody. What he was saying was a mystery to the porter; he was probably telling everyone of his financial problems. After his speech, he walked up and down the passageway of the train with his hat held out, hoping to get some change.

It was now only a matter of time before Luca met up with his old friend from the good old days. He was sweating and standing in one of the train carriages in the Paris underground, and she was waiting patiently in a small room on the top floor of a Paris hotel. They were soon to meet yet again. They had said 'Hello' and 'Goodbye' many times before. It was like a film playback or an action replay. The porter continued to daydream, and now it was the time to daydream about the woman he was about to meet, yet again.

His mind once more wandered back in time, to when he was only nineteen years of age. He had just had his lung operation, a hospital experience the porter wished to forget. It was during his post-operation convalescence that he met Katherine for the first time; she had been only fifteen years of age. The young girl, day after day, would walk briskly down the garden path and knock on Luca's kitchen door. She was an outgoing type of girl, not afraid to talk or make new friends. Luca was at home, relaxing and taking it easy. He was still weak, and still wore the hospital bandages to cover the long scar on his back.

She came daily, firstly to take the little dog out for a walk, and then later, when Luca's niece was born, she came regularly to babysit. It was during these regular daily visits that Luca and the young girl got to know each other. Day by day, they became good friends.

As time passed and the years rolled on, the little girl grew up and became closer to the young man. She encouraged him to go swimming with her and they would go out together in the evenings. They would go for walks, and as soon as Katherine was old enough, they would go for drinks in the neighbourhood pubs.

Now the underground train was speeding ahead. The porter was sweating profusely, as all this walking and running around, pulling his luggage behind him was draining him. The Paris metro was, for the amateur, a real maze to get through. It was not only physically exhausting, but also mentally demanding. On a few occasions, the porter was actually lost. He came out of the underground to find out that he was at the wrong station, so he had to return, buy a new ticket and go down to the trains via steps, corridors and elevators, get on another train and get off at the next stop. However, after so much running and walking, after paying special attention to the underground map, available for all to see above in the train's notice boards, situated above the passengers' heads, the porter at last arrived at the right station. He looked out of the train window to read the name of the station, and as soon as the double doors opened, he walked out on to the platform amongst the other commuters, who were rushing and pushing past him.

The Paris metro was dreary and dull. People were all dressed in autumn clothing, as the weather was very wet outside, up on the Paris streets. The porter walked and walked, turned left then right, climbed some steps, walked along more subways and went up the escalator until he saw the road sign he was looking for: Rue Carnot. That was the street name for the hotel where he was going to meet his friend. He kept on following the signs until finally he went through two glass doors, which opened up to the street outside. He climbed the steps with some difficulty, but finally got out of the underground and on to a major Parisian avenue.

It was now dark outside, but there were so many lights on that it seemed like daylight. Street lamps and hotel neon signs, and shop and restaurant signs were all switched on. He had emerged from the underground, on to the surface, right in the centre of a major city. He looked around in bewilderment at first, but in the nearby distance he spotted a neon sign indicating the name of the hotel where he was supposed to be meeting his friend.

Reunion

Luca walked through the hotel doors and made his way to the reception desk. There was a concierge who seemed really world-weary and bored, at times even irritated, or slightly aggressive with the hotel clients. He seemed to hate his job. Luca asked the French concierge what room his companion was staying in, even though he already knew the room number. The Frenchman told him the room number and pointed towards the small lift, telling him at which floor to get off.

The lift was very small. Luca stepped into the lift with his suitcase and sports bag and pressed the top floor button. On the lift wall was a sign saying, 'On leaving the hotel, please leave your room keys at the reception.' How very well organised, Luca thought.

The hotel room, he had been told, was on the top floor. It was a room situated under the roof, like an attic room. It had great charm; it had the feel of being a Dutch hotel, with a sense of art in the air, even if there were no big paintings to be seen around. On reaching the top floor, the lift doors opened and Luca stepped out into a narrow corridor where all the walls and ceiling were coloured red. It was quite dark, but there was a dim light on, strong enough to illuminate the way to the rooms.

It felt very cosy, quiet, sheltered and dim. He was moments – just a few paces away – from meeting his companion. All he had to do was find the right door, and there it was: Room 406. The door was situated near the lift but round a corner and down a slight slope. It was surely the smallest room in the hotel, the last one available before the hotel declared itself full. It was comparable to Room 3 in the porter's own hotel in Sicily; it was the last room to be rented. If all the other hotel rooms were full, Room 3 would be available. It was the final option. In Sicily, Room 3 had no windows, but only a double door, which opened out on to a high wall, so the view was poor, practically non-existent. It was small and claustrophobic and therefore one of the most unwanted rooms; but it was good enough to sleep in, if that's all one wanted from a room. The furniture was black and antique. It was, in effect, the most difficult room to let, but not impossible. Well, Room 406 in the Paris hotel looked like one of those 'last resort' rooms. From its position partially out of sight in the corridor it certainly looked like it.

Luca put down his now heavy luggage and quietly knocked on the door. The door opened, slowly, and there, staring at Luca in an uneasy manner, was Katherine. She stared at him in wonder for a few seconds, and then tried to embrace and kiss him. They exchanged kisses on the cheeks, as Luca would not consent to more because he was, at that stage, sweating profusely. His clothes were saturated with sweat, as a result of all the running around he had been doing in the French underground.

He entered the room, bringing in his luggage, placing it where he could, as the room was very small. The woman had been lying on the bed, watching TV;

she was wearing a nightgown and was looking quite comfortable. She had spectacles on and had her hair tied back in a ponytail. The room was so small that there was only just room enough to walk around the bed. The TV and mini-fridge were crammed into a corner and there was a dressing table up against a window, through which one could look down on an internal square courtyard. Looking down below through the window, the room seemed very high up. The wardrobe was also crammed into a small corner; the tiny bathroom was directly opposite the bed. The door had frosted glass and was semi-transparent, so whoever sat on the toilet could be seen from the outside.

It was all quite cosy but small, so very small. The wallpaper was designed with roses, which surely helped one to tolerate the small room, to make it feel romantic but less claustrophobic. The room seemed designed on purpose for lovers, for whoever wanted to spend a passionate weekend in Paris. The floor creaked, and the walls were not very thick, as Luca later discovered. Inside the fridge there were some basic drinks and refreshments. On either side of the bed were a radio and telephone apparatus. In all, it seemed quaint.

Luca quickly undressed and got into the shower. He shut the glass sliding doors behind him and stood under the hot water, which he felt was a great relief. After the long journey from Rome, it was wonderful to be able to shower and clean up. The last time he'd seen a shower was in his friend's flat in Rome. He had left the Italian capital very early in the morning, and then spent the whole day on two different trains. Now he was in Paris, reunited with his old girlfriend, and it was about two o'clock in the morning. The train journey seemed incredibly long, especially with all the daydreaming Luca had gone through, but now he was with Katherine, he was no longer alone with his thoughts, he now had someone to talk to, to exchange views feelings and sentiments. He was in Paris now, and the journey was not over yet, but the worst, and most alarming part of the trip seemed over. Luca could shower and wash away not only the sweat of a hard journey, but also some of the fear and anxiety connected to it.

Luca washed, dried and put on clean clothing. He then let himself flop down on the bed, exhausted. His companion did not lose any time before kissing and hugging him in a warm amorous embrace. They lay there, hardly believing that they were together again after such a long time. They talked about the journey; they drank and occasionally glanced at the TV, which was still showing a French film. After they fervently made love, their exhaustion was so great that they both fell asleep, forgetting to switch off the lights. It was stimulating to be in Paris, to be in a hotel, in a tiny room on the top floor.

The couple had been living separate lives for twenty years, yet there they were, waking up together in a French hotel room, as if the twenty years had never been. It was their desire to relive the happier moments of their lives, their wish to replay them all over again. In fact the first night together seemed strange but normal. Was it reality, or was Luca having another daydreaming episode? This time it was reality. Luca was not on the Starship Enterprise, beaming down on a lost planet in the universe to visit a friend he had not seen for years; he was not travelling in a time machine and visiting a companion in her world and time.

He was not dreaming, it was all real. The hotel, the room, and his old girlfriend who looked pretty much the same as she did twenty years ago. Luca had grey hair now, but Katherine looked exactly the same. Luca was confused: was this reality or dream, dream or reality? Was he really in Paris, with the grey sky up above? Would he wake up now, get up and go for a cycle ride along the beach in sunny Sicily? It was all quite confusing, but Luca continued as if nothing was happening – or going to happen – which would make him fall in a state of fear again. Dream or reality, he thought, let it be, *che sará sará*.

The room was definitely the smallest one in the hotel; they didn't have much room to manoeuvre. The floorboards creaked under the thick red carpet, but the rose-printed wallpaper made the room acceptable and less like a prison cell. It was cosy inside, whilst outside the weather was typically cold, grey and wintry. Luca and his companion went down to the hotel restaurant to have their breakfast. The restaurant was delightfully decorated. It was painted in an ancient Roman interior decoration style, with Roman statues here and there. The pair sat at a round table and the French waitress promptly came to take their orders. A few minutes later, a full French breakfast was served: bread, butter, croissants, toast with tea and coffee, and orange juice and yoghurts. They sat and ate and talked. At other tables in the restaurant, businessmen were eating their breakfast and reading the morning newspapers.

After breakfast, the couple decided to see the French capital; they wanted to spend a couple of days in the city before continuing with their journey north to Ireland. They left the hotel and started to stroll around. The hotel was in a good position; it was near the Arc de Triomphe and the Champs-Élysées. The Eiffel Tower was very close too. It was their first visit to the famous tower. As they walked towards the tower, the landmark seemed to get taller and taller. It was a great sight, a grand feeling to be able to stand beneath the tall structure. There were tourists everywhere, taking photographs, queuing up to get on the lift to take them up the tower. Virtually the whole day was spent walking in the vicinity of the tower. It was a joyful experience.

The second day was much the same as the first. Further monuments were visited, and the couple walked for miles, sometimes walking round in circles. They walked over the main bridges, in wide open parkland and down long, wide avenues. They looked at shops and walked until their feet were sore, until it was dark.

On the third day they both decided it was the right moment to leave and head north to Ireland. That morning they quickly packed their cases, went down to the restaurant to have their breakfast, and sat at the table for the last time. Luca made sure he ate everything that was brought to him on the table by the ponytailed French waitress. They soon finished eating and got up to leave. They returned to their small room for the last time, collected their cases, locked the door with the key on their way out and made their way out into the avenue, after having paid the receptionist at the desk.

Cherbourg

Outside the hotel they got on a bus, which took them to the St Lazare train station. There they bought the train tickets for Cherbourg, the French port situated on the north coast of France, on the Normandy coast.

They got on the train, and soon it was making its way out of the station and the French capital.

Once the train was far out into the countryside, Luca and Katherine could see swampy fields all around them. The countryside seemed waterlogged. It was in that very area that the Allies made their move inland towards Paris after the well-known D-Day landings on the Normandy beaches.

As the train raced along the railway track, Luca listened intently to the rhythmic noise of the train's wheels rolling along the tracks. He gradually heard the sound of machine guns firing and hand grenades exploding. He saw an armada of American and British ships approaching the French shores. He could hear the sound of bullets whizzing close by and thudding and whipping through the surface of the sea. Luca could visualise images of the invading, liberating soldiers jumping off their boats, helplessly being hit, maimed or killed by the hammering bullets and bombs. He could see their bleeding severed limbs scattered all over the Normandy beaches. He could almost imagine the dreadful fear the soldiers must have felt before getting mercilessly executed by the enemy. War! Trenches! Bombs! Man killing man! What madness and insanity, Luca thought.

The train only took about three hours to get to Cherbourg. Before reaching the station, Luca caught sight of the sea; it was a grey dull colour, just like the sky above them, and the horizon could not be easily distinguished, as the sky and sea seemed to merge together.

The big ferry was waiting in the port. It looked enormous. The green shamrock symbol could be clearly seen on the ship's funnel. A flag – green, white and orange in colour – could be seen at the back end of the ship, waving at the end of a tall white pole.

Once off the train, the couple got a taxi, which took them directly to the ship's terminal building. After waiting in the spacious building, Luca and Katherine went through passport control. They exhibited their documents to a uniformed French officer who kindly let them through the gateway and long corridor, then on to a long coach which, when full and ready, set off and took all the passengers directly on to the ferry. The passengers then got off and made their way up from the car deck to the upper passenger decks.

Katherine soon made her way to the reception desk to book a small cabin for the both of them. On her return with the keys, they both made their way to the central decks at the back end of the ship, and looked for their little cabin. When they found it, they entered and found two bunk beds and a small bathroom, shower included. A door from another cabin somewhere in the vicinity was banging noisily and repetitively; the ship's swaying movement was causing it to do so. Luca thought it might bang all night if that cabin remained empty throughout the journey.

After settling down in their mini-cabin, having cleaned washed and changed, they both decided to take a look around the three-levelled ship.

They walked out into the corridor and made their way up the main stairs to the upper levels. The top level was where the door opened out on to the outside deck. There were lots of people there already, walking about from one end of the ship to the other; others were standing at the top deck's protective railings, looking down at the water level, which was a hundred metres below. Luca looked down too and could see the agitated waters caused by the ship's engine and propellers; the noise was deafening. There was a slight wind in the port area, but that was just a taste of the gale force winds that were out at sea. The sea was quite calm in the Cherbourg port, but looking out on the horizon Luca could see that the water was not so serene. Luca was not very optimistic, and deep down he was not looking forward to spending the next eighteen hours at sea.

As the ship started to move out of the port and into the wide open sea, the couple went downstairs to the lower internal decks, where it was warmer. There they went to the buffet restaurant and decided to have something to eat and drink. They sat a table near a very big window, which overlooked the stern of the boat, so, as the ship sailed, they could watch the white and grey spray of the agitated waters in the ship's wake.

After they'd eaten they got up and walked around the ship to have a better look at the other decks. There

Cherbourg

was a coffee shop, a bar or pub with adequate seating, which allowed a good view of a stage, which occasionally had live musical bands playing on it. The stage was also sometimes used for dancing.

There was a play area for children, and a games room with all the latest electronic machines. There was a souvenir shop, a seating area for TV viewers, and small banks and exchange offices just in case you wanted to exchange your money. There was a classy restaurant, which catered for the big spenders.

The ship had all you needed for a short journey. It was not quite as big as a cruise liner, but it was comfortable, except for the swaying of the ship, which was beginning to make life unpleasant for Katherine. She soon started to complain of feeling seasick.

They went back to their cabin and she stayed in the cabin for the rest of the journey. The more the ship ventured out into the open sea, the rougher and higher were the waves.

The door that had been banging earlier on had stopped. Someone from the ship's personnel must have come and closed the door. It would have been hell to have to listen to a continuous banging all night long, as well as putting up with the ship's rocking movement. Luca and Katherine could feel every wave, every crest and trough, every up and down. It felt as if they were on a plane, as if there was a very strong turbulence; but rather than being strapped to a seat, they were free to walk around the cabin and the ship. They were free to walk the perilous outer deck. They could have fun balancing and counterbalancing for the next eighteen hours. The majority of the passengers

Cherbourg

walked around the boat looking like drunken people on a Saturday night, unable to walk in a straight line. Katherine decided to stay in the cabin for the rest of the journey. For her the sea crossing was very long indeed.

For the rest of the evening Luca came and went. He walked around the ship on his own. He sat at the ship's bar and drank. Later on in the evening, some people were brave enough to test their stomachs by having tea or supper. The restaurants filled up, as did the buffet and coffee shop.

Later, the passengers slowly dwindled; some went to their cabins, others just sat on any seat available and made themselves comfortable. When it got late, and the ship began to look empty, Luca went back to his cabin, to his ailing partner.

The vessel continued to pound the troughs of the waves, then take off like a bird, then thump the base again, continuously. Luca found this to be an interesting experience, but his companion swore that she would never set foot on a ship again.

When Luca got back to his cabin, he found that Katherine was already undressed and lying in her bunk bed; she did not look very well and was pale in the face. Luca closed the door behind him and locked it; he undressed and climbed the small ladder that was on the side of the bunk beds. The top bed was ready for use, blankets and cushions were already in place, and all he had to do was undress and lie down. He lay on the bed and switched the lights off. There they were, in the dim cabin, in a small tight space, experiencing what was most definitely a rough ride.

Cherbourg

The ups and downs of the boat went on throughout the night. With every up motion, they could sense and envisage the ship trying to take off from the runway, which in this case was the sea. At every up movement, it felt just like a plane about to take off, then, instead of taking off, the big vessel plunged downwards, and they could imagine and visualise the ship slicing into the hard, heavy agitated waters of the sea. Then, rather than heading downwards continuously, like a plane that is about to descend, the ship encountered resistance and was then pushed back upwards, as if it had hit a gigantic trampoline, or sponge.

Luca's body was not exactly in accord with the ship's movements. His body felt as if it wanted to glide, to float, as if it were in space, above the earth's atmosphere. Luca's body did not move up and down in unison with the ship, as one body. There was a few retarded moments' delay, and in those few moments his body was afloat for a split second, as if separated from the vessel. Katherine, too, was feeling the unpleasant ups and downs of the ship, but she was lying there, with her eyes closed, quietly bearing this undesirable voyage.

Luca definitely could not sleep; he lay there with his eyes wide open, gazing at the cabin ceiling, which was close to his face. He was, in an unconventional way, enjoying his voyage. He just lay there wondering what lay ahead, wondering again where he was travelling from, and where he was travelling to.

Nothing in particular happened during the night. The sleepless traveller left the cabin and wandered out on the ship's decks. Most of the other passengers had retired to their own cabins, so there was nobody about. Luca walked around on his own, listening attentively to all the ship's noises, the sounds of metal and wood creaking. He walked round the vessel as if on an athletics circuit. The bar and souvenir shop was now closed; the restaurant, coffee shop, and buffet bar were also closed for the night. The only room open was the games room, where all the electronic machines were; but even there, there was nobody about.

The porter and the ship were alone together, just like the porter and his hotel. At night, he had the whole ship to himself. He felt at ease, comfortable. He was alone, only this time he was not lying down on a padded deckchair, in the small boxroom at his hotel. He walked round and round in circles, observing every particular feature of the ship, looking at every empty seat in the lounge and restaurant. It all looked and felt so different. The sense of void and emptiness was strong, but it was quiet and peaceful. Luca looked out of the window and could see nothing, as it was very dark, except for the flashing light from a distant lighthouse, which seemed to be located in the middle of the sea, but was probably located on a rock at England's Land's End. After he had finished checking the situation, he went back to his cabin, to his companion, who was still sleeping, still feeling unpleasant.

The morning came, and Luca was restless, he could not remain in the cabin for very long, it was claustrophobic. He got dressed and had a quick wash in the rocking bathroom. The ship's movements of the previous night were the same; nothing in the boat's movements had changed, and it was still difficult to balance oneself, to walk in a straight line. The sea was still a little agitated. He opened the door and walked out of the cabin. He decided to take another stroll around the ship. He looked out of the window and he could see the sea for miles around. There was still no sight of land, but the sea and sky still looked dull and grey.

He went back to the cabin to see if Katherine was all right, if she was still asleep. She was awake and feeling a little better, but she swore that she would never go on a ship again. Luca encouraged her to get up, to get herself ready. If she was better, he said, they could go and have a coffee.

Soon they were both out and walking around the ship, which was now more crowded. All the passengers were up, eager to get breakfast in the restaurant or in the coffee and buffet bar. Some people were already sitting at their tables, with an abundant full Irish breakfast in front of them: sausages, black pudding, bacon, eggs and baked beans were spilling over some of the plates. Some people had a simple toast, some just an espresso. Luca and his companion settled for a simple coffee and croissant. They sat at a table and quietly consumed their breakfast.

After breakfast, they went to the top outer deck. The sun had come out, but the sea was still rough, and it was still very windy. In the distance other ships could be seen, and there was a very thin black line on the horizon. It was too cold and windy to stay on the top deck, so they returned inside and sat near the portholes. They observed the thin black line. It was

Cherbourg

land; it was Ireland. Soon, their eighteen-hour crossing would be over, soon they would be on solid, firm land, which would be a joy and liberation for Katherine.

Surprisingly, the weather was improving. The overcast cloudy sky was clearing. The land was slowly getting bigger as the ship approached it. It was no longer a thin black line on the horizon any more; it was now an extensive green terrain. At regular intervals, standing on *terra firma*, there were slim, high windmills, with their long thin blades revolving in the wind. There must have been ten of them in a row. It looked as if the ship was approaching Amsterdam in Holland, not Rosslare in Ireland.

The passengers on the top outer deck stood at the railings to look at the land approaching. It was a sight to fill the eyes. Slowly but surely all the little details got bigger and bigger, they could begin to see the roads and houses and cars. It was a great feeling to see dry land again. The people on the ship were not alone any more; there were more people out there, on land. Gradually the passengers started to move towards the ship's exit doors. Luca and Katherine made their way back to their cabin after hearing the voice on the loudspeaker telling everyone to prepare for disembarkation. They got their luggage ready and made their way back into the main assembly area of the ship, and gathered with the other passengers at the stated meeting points.

The passengers were instructed to go down the exit stairs and make their way off the ship. Luca and Katherine joined and followed the line of people leaving the ship, all lined one behind the other in an

Cherbourg

orderly fashion. After crossing a ramp, which led them off the ship on to the land, they all walked down a very long tunnel. They went through passport control. The Irish and British nationals were allowed to go straight through without any problems, but some non-European nationals were stopped for more severe questioning and checks.

Luca and Katherine had British passports, so they were allowed through without hindrance. One more short tunnel and a ramp, and the passengers were out into the main terminal building, where parents and relatives, if any, would be waiting to collect them.

Ireland

The long journey was nearly over, for the porter and his companion only had a few more miles to go before getting to her home. Luca saw a mysterious young woman, possibly in her late teens, outside the terminal building, waiting in trepidation to drive the couple north to County Kildare.

Luca had left Sicily on a sunny, warm day. He was now in Ireland with Katherine, and to his surprise it was also a bright sunny day here. The drive from the Irish port of Rosslare to Katherine's home was not very far, but immediately Luca was taken aback by the beautiful, tidy green countryside he could see out of the car window. He was amazed to see such wide open spaces. He still had Sicily in his mind, with all the rugged barren hills and mountains, some steep, some gentle, with the brooding Mount Etna dominating them all. He thought of all the villages with their houses, side by side, and the narrow streets. He thought of the temperamental ground beneath his feet on the Mediterranean island, the constant threat of earthquakes. He thought how different it was in Ireland, what a contrast. The green land was continually fed with abundant rainfall, and was generally always settled and calm, with no molten lava beneath the surface waiting to burst to the exterior, no sudden underground movements to shake the living daylights out of you.

Although tourists generally described Sicily to be like paradise, to the porter, Ireland was also like paradise. Sicily had the blue summer skies and deep blue sea, and above all the higher temperatures, whereas Ireland had the picturesque, luscious carpet-like green pastures. Sicily was a world of blues; Ireland was a world of greens, each of them two different worlds, two different kinds of bliss.

It was a pleasant revelation. Luca had expected a gloomy, dull place, but instead it was quite the opposite. It looked colourful, tranquil and peaceful, blessed by the infrequent sunshine. The roads looked immediately clean and neat and well signposted. The Irish traffic seemed to be so controlled and the drivers well behaved. The houses looked tidy and appealing, the colours were pleasing, and they were more often than not low-lying bungalows with a good plot of land around them. It was the great open spaces that surprised Luca the most. It was as if he was suddenly let out of a prison cell, simply because everybody in Ireland seemed to be surrounded by so much space – some gardens were the size of a soccer pitch.

He didn't see one house that was uncompleted or that was in need of a revamp; every home was well looked after, kept tidy, neat and always well painted. This was a contrast to Sicily, where many occupied or uninhabited houses seemed to require urgent, drastic repairs, or even completion. Was this an indication of different mentality between the two peoples? Perhaps one was careless and neglectful, the other industrious and proud... or was there a difference in the two countries' economic condition?

Ireland

Luca was finally in Ireland; his long journey was almost ended. The long train journey, which was perhaps supposed to have given him many new adventures, many new opportunities of meeting new people, had instead given him the opportunity to go back in time, to relive some moments of his past life. He had arrived in this new world where Katherine had been living for the last twenty years, whilst he was over 2,000 kilometres away in Sicily. She had promised to show him her new home, her new life, her new surroundings.

After a couple of hours driving northwards toward Dublin, they were nearly home. The young, mysterious teenage girl sitting in the driver's seat drove them along very long, straight roads, with tall trees on either side. The fields were thronged with sheep or cows. The roads were particularly narrow at times, with a small narrow ditch on either side. The ditches were, as his companion alleged, quite dangerous. A driver's slight miscalculation or distraction meant that the whole car could end up in the ditch. It had happened to her, Katherine remarked. 'Best to keep the eyes on the road at all times... Keep the wheel on the asphalt, don't go on the mud with the wheel, or else the car will be sucked into the ditch, and that could be fatal.'

The porter could see how dangerous it was. The drivers seemed to be accustomed to the long narrow roads; at times the space between the cars going in opposite directions was minimal. Either a driver goes slightly more to the right and hits an oncoming vehicle, or he goes slightly to the left and end up in a deep muddy trench. At first sight, the drivers in this country seemed quite good, with a precise eye for the roads. They travelled at high speeds. Sometime, great big lorries appeared on the road ahead. The porter kept his mouth shut, but was thinking that the end was nigh. The lorries moved fast and took up half of the road's width. When the lorries approached and passed their car going in the opposite direction, the space between the two vehicles was minute. A few centimetres further out, and a head-on collision was a certainty.

Luca reflected for one second on his own dangerous driving experience. He recalled the time when as a young man, he and his three friends had gone on a holiday from England to Sicily and back by car, a journey of approximately 4,000 kilometres. Luca and his friends were driving a beautiful 2.5cc English saloon car with comfortable seats, wooden-looking panels, and a sporty style dashboard. On the gearstick there was a small button, which, if pressed, would have put the car in its highest gear. Luca remembered the last few miles of their long, tiring homeward journey back to England. They had been travelling for two and a half days and were all exhausted. They took it in turns to drive during the day and through most of the night.

It was three o'clock in the morning and Luca was driving fast on the empty three-carriage motorway. His companions were fast asleep. Luca was also tired and sleepy but he knew they were nearly home, he knew that they only had thirty kilometres to go. The headlights were on full beam and the road seemed all clear. Suddenly, out of nowhere, Luca saw something in his path. He rubbed his tired eyes to see better but could only distinguish a grey mass in the middle of the road, in his lane. He couldn't tell what it was, he couldn't see the object clearly, but he immediately thought it was a dead animal, perhaps a dog or a horse. The car was travelling at such a high speed that Luca really had no time or distance to slow down or avoid it. If he had tried to steer out of the object's path he might have hit it with the car's left or right wheel and sent the vehicle flying into a ditch. He had to think quickly, and all he could do was hit the mysterious object straight on, hoping that the object was soft and low enough to avoid hitting the underside of the car. The closer the car got to the object, the less low and soft the entity appeared. It no longer looked like a dead animal, but more like a metallic object, like a television set or a car engine that must have fallen off the back of a lorry.

Luca powerlessly and unavoidably hit the object at full speed. The car hit the object with a jolt, then scrambled over it with a loud clang and rattle, then, surprisingly, continued to go forward in a straight line. The sleeping friends were suddenly awakened by the thump, wondering what had happened.

The car continued normally for a few miles till it coughed to a stop. The radiator had been ripped open and all the cooling liquid had escaped, causing the engine to burn up in white smoke.

The first few days were spent settling down in his companion's little house, situated in a little village about two hours from Dublin. Luca had to get used to the new house and the garden, with its green grass, which was like a thick indoor carpet.

Ireland

It was a quiet neighbourhood. During the day, after the children had gone to school, and their parents to work, nobody could be seen. It was quiet. This silence seemed very agreeable to Luca. The view from the window, of open fields, and open grass areas, seemed new and out of the ordinary. It was a peaceful spot, a great place to come home to at night. The views alone made him feel like a liberated man, the sense of space filled his sight and mind. For an instant, Luca thought back to his home in Sicily, to the main Messina to Catania road, with the noise of the traffic, day in and day out, going up and down the street. The incessant noise of engines of all types would be roaring in front of his bedroom window. The sound was particularly intense between five in the afternoon and nine in the evening. What made things worse was the fact that his house had no front garden; the doors and windows opened directly on to a narrow footpath, then on to the road itself. To add to the noise was the passing of the train on the railway lines, only metres away from the back of the house. The house was practically sandwiched between the railway and the highway. The noise, therefore, was part of the scenery, part of the house. What respite it was to experience the silence of his companion's home! It was situated in a cul-de-sac, and there were open fields in the distance, with cows roaming about on them. Nearby, round the corner and on the main road leading to Dublin, were a church and cemetery, a few shops and a petrol station. The noise of traffic was restricted to that area.

Katherine had a black and white dog, a collie, that had the whole back garden to roam around in. Luca thought of his black cat that he had been feeding in Sicily. He wondered where it would go to find food, once the creature had noticed the porter was no longer there to feed him his daily ration of biscuits.

So Luca had to get used to the new environment, the new TV stations, the new climate. After a couple of days of settling in her home and making everything perfectly comfortable for Luca, his girlfriend had to return to her duties as a teacher. She had to go back to work, and her work meant she had to travel for miles to different towns and villages throughout Ireland. It meant long hours of driving; it meant she had to get up early in the morning, around five and work all day, and only get home at nine in the evening. Luca saw she had become a hard worker, far removed from the teenage girl or young woman who used to walk down the garden path to visit the young man, her neighbour, so many years ago.

Luca was invited to go with her wherever she taught; he would take a walk in the town whilst she was in the classroom. He would explore these new places, walking for hours, in and out of all the streets, looking at all the shops. They would meet during her tea break, and go together to sit in a bar or coffee shop. At the end of the day they would meet up and get in the car to drive home.

Day after day Luca went with his companion, he was getting his fill of sightseeing. He saw the famous bog area, where the Irish cut, dry and collect the turf, the earthy material that they use to burn as fuel in their fireplaces. Further afield he saw the Wicklow Mountains, with all their peaks and meadows, just like those in the postcards that he'd received through the post whilst he was in Sicily. It all looked very picturesque.

Luca had his camera with him, and when he thought there was a good photo to take, he took it. They went to Bray, by the Irish Sea, and to Dingle on the west coast. She took him to Limerick, Port Laoise, Mullingar, Cavan, Drogheda and Tullamore.

It was tiring at times. At the beginning of it all Luca had left Sicily by train and had travelled the whole length of Italy, and gone through the Alps to cross the whole of France. He had spent eighteen hours crossing the sea; and finally he travelled all over Ireland by car. It was definitely exhausting. He was on the move all the time.

Luca's holiday started to stretch out in time. From the day he'd left Sicily, to the days in which he was now exploring Ireland, a month had passed unnoticed. Luca and Katherine were getting to know each other again, without realising it. The twenty years that had divided them seemed to evaporate gradually, and at times it all seemed back to normal, it seemed as if they'd gone back in time; but that was not the reality. The reality was that they had both travelled through time, matured, and they were perhaps different people altogether.

Occasionally Luca and Katherine went out in the evenings. They visited a few hotel bars and had a few drinks, like they used to do twenty years ago. They went for meals in Italian or Chinese restaurants and occasionally to Irish restaurants. Luca was getting his fill of Chinese food and fish and chips. In Sicily, Chinese restaurants were rare, although they were not impossible to find. As for fish and chips, well, in Sicily they were not quite the same. They did not smell and taste the same and were not as greasy as in England or Ireland. Not a great healthy meal, true, but Luca liked the smell and taste of freshly cooked spuds from a chip shop. They reminded him of his youth. They reminded him of the bag of chips bought when he and his mates came out of the swimming baths and had finished their games lesson at school. All they wanted, after spending an hour in the tepid water and chlorine-filled swimming pool, and getting out into the bitter cold air into the freezing teeth-chattering dressing rooms, was a steaming, vinegar-smelling bag of piping hot golden chips.

It was just like a soundtrack played on the radio, of an oldie like Elvis Presley, or the Beatles, which can remind many people of their past; similarly the bag of chips transported Luca back in time. The steak and kidney pie too, took Luca back to the days when he used to go with his father in the car late at night to deliver new work to the trouser-maker. His father used to stop on the way, in a nice pub, and go in and buy a hot, steaming steak and kidney pie. Every time Luca ate a pie, it reminded him of the few fond moments he'd spent in the company of his father, the few moments he could spend with him, when his father was not busy with a needle and thread, sewing away at his suits and jackets, from morning to night.

Time passed unnoticed. The days went by, and all Luca could do was to continue to go with Katherine, in the car, to all her places of work. Sometimes they travelled in the dark, mostly along straight and narrow roads. Sometimes they didn't get home till ten o'clock at night. When they did get home, the barking collie would be faithfully awaiting them inside the house. Luca would set the stove, place the brick-shaped sods of grey turf in the fire and set it alight. Slowly but gradually, the small flicker of flame at the end of a matchstick would flare into a fast flame, creating an impressive glow, a dancing spectacle of fire, behind the small glass shutter.

Staring at the stove and the flames whilst his companion prepared the spaghetti and garlic at the kitchen, Luca thought back to the time he had started fires accidentally. The first fire was when he was little. He had turned on the electric fire in the front room of his house, hoping to heat the house for his working parents. But the fire was placed too near the curtains. It was only after an hour, when a neighbour had come knocking on the front door in a frantic manner, that Luca and his older sister realised that their front room was on fire. All the curtains and wooden windows were ablaze. Outside the house there was a small group of people watching the spectacle. The fire brigade eventually put out the fire, but it was a tragedy for Luca. He hated the thought of his parents coming home to that fiery scene.

Sometimes Luca stayed at home. He read books and he tried his best to kill time when he was alone at home. He sometimes took the dog out for long walks.

Luca knew that his time in Ireland was nearly up; he'd been away from home for two months now. Soon he would be receiving phone calls from his employers to tell him that the new season was just around the

Ireland

corner and that he would have to start work again. He knew that his time of liberty, his adventure, was nearly over. He was not, in fact, keen to start thinking about his long homeward journey, yet again by train; yet again facing the fears of another long voyage.

On a quiet Sunday morning, when Luca and Katherine were still sleeping, Luca's phone rang. Luca answered the mobile phone. It was his mother telling him to get in touch with the manager, his employer. Soon afterwards, Luca rang his manager, but the manager's wife, the hotel secretary, answered the phone. 'It's time you started work,' she said. 'You are due to start at the beginning of the month.'

The porter replied, 'I... I am still in Ireland. I couldn't get a train ticket yet. Could you give me another week?'

The secretary wanted to help, so she agreed to give the porter another week to sort out his ticket problem.

The week quickly passed and Luca still didn't have any train tickets. He usually bought them on the way, as he was travelling.

Not only was Luca a little reluctant to make his homeward journey, to face the usual travel fears, but he was strangely hesitant to leave his rediscovered companion. She was reluctant to let him go too. During the last week, before he had to get in touch with his manager again to say he was on his way, there was a period of sentimental upheavals and pressures, which Luca shared with his companion. It was very much like their last week of life, as if they were condemned to death and they were both 'dead men walking' down the corridor before an execution of one or both of them. Their time together seemed as if it was never going to finish, but the end of the holiday had arrived for Luca. He had to leave, but leaving was now very difficult. It was like putting an end to a fairy tale. 'Don't leave; please don't go! Stay here,' was the constant and recurrent plea that Katherine made to Luca.

As each day passed, it was a day too close to the end. It was a black day on a calendar. Luca and Katherine tried to apply the brakes to the time that was ticking away. When they went out and drove around in the car they dismissed the last day as if it never existed. When they went shopping, they pretended that all was normal, that they had all the time in the world.

What could he say this time? What could he tell the secretary so that she would extend his time for another week? Or better still, till the beginning of the new month? Could he tell her he was ill, and couldn't make the journey?

As they were driving in the Limerick area in the south-west of Ireland, a phone call came in and Katherine answered. The voice on the speaker was loud and clear; it was Luca's mother.

'The manager phoned this morning, sounding furious. He said if you are not at work by the beginning of next month, you will lose your job!' His mother sounded concerned and distressed. 'I advise you to ring him as soon as possible – sort it out!'

Luca's blood pressure must have risen suddenly. His adrenalin started to flow in his veins, as he knew that if he phoned the manager, his and his manager's temper would erupt. Luca unwillingly dialled his hotel number in Sicily, as his girlfriend was still at the wheel, driving the car. After a couple of ring tones, the manager answered the phone.

'Hello, I'm the night porter, calling from Ireland. I heard you wanted to speak to me!'

The manager replied in a grating voice 'When are you coming back? If you are not back here at your post, here at the hotel, on duty on the first night of the beginning of the month, you are fired! Understood?' He spoke in his usual enraged, aggressive tone of voice. He was the type of person who spoke in a hostile, aggressive manner to all of his subordinates. The urge to answer back in an equally angry tone was very strong, but the porter knew how to control himself.

'Yes, OK, I will try to leave on the next boat as soon as possible. I will be there, don't worry!'

It sounded very much like a submission on Luca's part, but it was just a way of avoiding any further telephone aggression. He knew his manager, knew what he was like, and did not want to waste his breath arguing. The phone call was very brief and ended abruptly.

Luca and Katherine were dumbfounded at the tone of voice used by the manager. They sat there in silence for a few minutes, as she continued to drive to her work in the quiet green serenity of western Ireland.

'Well, that's it. I have to go, I can't stay in Ireland any longer,' the porter said. They both remained in silence for the rest of the journey, till they got home late at night.

Southbound

The following day, the porter started to study his route back. He firstly had to decide which day of the week he had to leave to coincide with the date of the Rosslare to Cherbourg ferry crossing; it ran about three times a week. His companion was still fixed in her thoughts. She did not want him to leave, to go back to Sicily, to leave for another twenty years, before seeing him again. It was too much for her to allow. She didn't want to face more lonely nights at home on her own, her and her dog between the four walls. But Luca had no choice.

Luca had three departure dates worked out, any one of which would have got him back at the hotel in time to start work. He prepared his luggage and was ready to go. It was early in the morning. She was ready to drive him to the southern port of Rosslare, a three-hour drive by car. They sat there in the living room for a while. The time started ticking away. The last half hour before the departure deadline was soul-destroying. It was again like the last half hour of life. The final fifteen minutes were even worse. Luca's blood pressure was surely at its peak. He just really was not ready yet, was not sure yet that he wanted to embark on another solitary journey.

If Luca and Katherine did not leave at that precise moment, Luca would miss his boat crossing. It was hard to leave. To make that split decision. The minutes rolled by and the deadline had arrived. It was now or next time. Leave now, or in two days' time. If not in two days, leave in six days' time. But leave, he had to.

The minutes passed over the deadline, and Luca could not bring himself to go. Ten minutes past the deadline, and still the porter could not persuade himself to go. It was intense, really intense. Was it the fear of the journey ahead, or the dread of separating from Katherine, who had been by his side for the last two months? Was it a fear of jumping into twenty years of emptiness and worthlessness again? The minutes continued to hurry by, and the time to get to the port was getting tight. If more time were wasted, he would have to abort his journey and leave after two more days.

The journey to the port by car was cancelled, and Luca could look forward to another forty-eight hours in Ireland with his woman, except that he was just prolonging the agony. At the end of the two extra days, again the deadline approached. That morning, luggage ready, the porter and his girlfriend were again looking at the clock, at the watch, at whatever told the time, they looked at it, hoping that the time would freeze, would stop. Once more, deep depression gripped both of them as their physical and mental separation was due yet again.

Katherine was suffering once again. She hated to be put through such mental and emotional strain. It was torture. She could not stand it any longer. With courage and decisiveness and with a very straight and solemn, heartbroken face she said, 'Come on, let's go. It's really time to go and say goodbye.'

Luca grabbed his luggage and put it in the boot of

Southbound

the car, then sat in the passenger seat. Katherine locked the house door and sat in the driver's seat. They reversed out of the drive and set off south, in the direction of the port.

After three hours' driving, during which the two of them sat together in absolute silence, not saying a word to each other, they arrived in Rosslare. The sea was out there in front of them, the view was good, and the weather was good. Katherine parked the car in the port car park, and when they finally stopped and she switched the engine off, they both sat there, as if stunned by an electric shock.

Their last moment together had come yet again. A tear or two could be seen on Katherine's face. She was desperately upset, and very sad and emotional. Luca too was sad, but now he wondered what to do. She was making it extremely difficult for him to cut the ties and leave. He was becoming weak willed, as he hated to see her cry, with tears slowly but surely cascading down the side of her face. She was getting more upset by the minute.

' Please don't go, please. Please don't leave, please, I love you, please stay here,' she pleaded.

Luca's throat became uncomfortable. He too was sad that he was leaving, but now he was having extreme difficulty in opening the car door. He had to think of something to release the emotional tension that was created by the both of them. How could he get away? How could he leave and get on the ship, which was already taking on the passengers bound for France?

After half an hour of crying and weeping, after her emotional strength started to break and become weaker, Luca made a move. He opened the car door and then persuaded his depressed companion to gather her strength and open the boot, so that he could get hold of his luggage. Katherine reluctantly did as he asked, and together they made their way to the port's passenger acceptance hall. There he quickly bought a ferry ticket at the ticket office, whilst she looked at him, not believing what was going on, not believing he was leaving yet again, leaving her perhaps for good, this time for the last time.

They made their way up a flight of steps and along a corridor to what looked like a tunnel entrance. It was the entrance to the ship reserved for passengers only. At this point they had to say goodbye. Luca never thought it would be the last goodbye, but his companion always did. She was tense, as if turned into stone. She looked very pale and upset. She stood there, frail and helpless, as he turned round to look her in the eyes, looking deep into her mind and soul.

'Goodbye, love,' he said in a low, cheerless voice. 'It's time for me to go.'

'Please don't!' she replied, in a last attempt to stop him.

'Don't worry; you come to see me in Sicily if you wish, it's not the end of the world.'

He quickly kissed her on the cheeks and lips, then briskly grabbed his suitcase and bag, turned and walked through the tunnel. He walked up a ramp, then round a corner till he was out of her sight. The break was rapid.

Southbound

Luca was already familiar with the ship, so he quickly made his way to the upper decks. He went immediately to the reception desk to book his little cabin, and once he'd received the keys, he briskly went to the cabin to deposit his suitcase and sports bag. This time the cabin had a quiet, solitary, tomb-like atmosphere. It didn't feel as inviting and friendly as it had on the northbound voyage. With his luggage safe, he closed and locked the cabin door and quickly made his way to the top outer deck. Again, many people were walking around the deck, looking around and standing at the railings.

The porter quickly tried to find a space to stand, where he could look out at the port area, at the passenger acceptance hall, and at the car park, where his girlfriend had parked the car. He strained his eyes to see her or the car, but he could not see anything at all amongst the many vehicles parked in the area. The first message came through on his mobile phone. The words appeared on his mobile screen: PLEASE COME BACK, DON'T GO, PLEASE. It was heartbreaking, but he had to ignore her. He kept on looking out at the car park, but to no avail.

The ship eventually but surely started to move. The propellers started to churn the cold, dark water and the ship started to vibrate as the vessel's engine roared. The car park on land started to look smaller and gradually became more distant. The messages kept on coming through to the porter: PLEASE GET OFF THE BOAT AND COME BACK. But it was too late. The ship was already moving away. With every second, it drew further and further away. The boat's speed built up and the car park eventually looked like a small thumbnail sketch on a big canvas. The porter replied to her messages, trying to give her words of comfort, but she insisted, PLEASE COME BACK, I LOVE YOU, PLEASE.

As the car park eventually looked like a black spot, the size of a pinhead, on the horizon, the messages on his mobile phone screen still came through with persistence. PLEASE COME BACK, I LOVE YOU. But the words that seemed to impact more on the heart and soul of the porter were her last words, just as the car park completely vanished out of sight, out of his vision:

I LOVE YOU, DON'T EVER FORGET IT!

Printed in the United Kingdom
by Lightning Source UK Ltd.
112855UKS00001BA/1